Promises

BAKER GIRL SERIES, BOOK 2

Mary Jane Forbes

Todd Book Publications

The Baker Girl Series

Book one:
One Summer

Book two:
Promises

What do an aspiring pastry chef, a wannabe cartoonist, and a mysterious reporter have in common—Charlie's Diner.

Pulled apart by events, distance, and life-long dreams, can promises given in the heat of passion be kept?

Prologue

STAR SPREAD A LARGE TOWEL on the warm Daytona Beach sand. Breathing in the salty air she gazed out over the horizon. No boats. No body-surfers. It was early. A jogger passed. Then a dog walker. Squinting, she tugged at her pink visor blocking the sun's brilliant rays. She dropped her yellow shirt, stretched out on the towel in her bikini, hands resting loosely on her stomach. Releasing a long sigh, a feeling of contentment washed over her body, the sound of the surf rolling gently up on the sand.

So peaceful.

Charlie's Diner, where she worked as a short-order cook over the summer, closed yesterday. Her Gran had urged her to take a few hours to decompress before tackling her plans to open a bakery.

The diner!

Her lips spread into a smile as she thought of all of her friends, the regulars at the diner. Benny, his wheelchair always giving him fits at the top of the handicap ramp as he struggled to navigate the diner's front door. *Note to self—make sure Benny can roll into the bakery.*

The Butterworth sisters … so much fun with their ever-changing T-shirts announcing a new diet, or new dance class, or new adventure.

Eyes closed, Star grinned thinking how lucky she was that Jane, who funded her courses in culinary arts at the local college, had frequented the diner for breakfast with her niece and her husband—Liz and Manny, private investigators. Star had known them only in passing, but over the summer the two PIs had helped big time with Ash.

Ash …

A brief summer crush? Her heart still skipped a beat thinking about him. But he had moved on, and she doubted she would see him again. They traded emails twice and that was it.

A scowl crossed her face remembering the filming of the TV reality series—Amateur Bakeoff Competition. She won the bakeoff but lost the money. The fifty-thousand-dollar grand prize never materialized, never awarded to her, thanks to Jim and Stephanie, the competition producers. What charlatans. Although … she was sure the producers didn't want the pilot TV show to end up the way it did. Still she desperately wanted to win the competition, win the money to finance a bakery business. The dream again elusive.

Elusive until a mysterious turn of events. Someone, an anonymous someone, left an envelope by the diner's cash register with her name it. After a busy shift cooking up meat tartlets with cranberry glaze, she had opened the envelope and found a check inside. A check made out to Star Bloom for a hundred thousand dollars. The thought of the check still sent shockwaves through her system. Who was anonymous? She hoped to find out someday.

She pushed up on her elbows hearing two little girls squeal as a chilly wave rolled over their toes. Sighing, Star turned over on her stomach, her idle thoughts returning.

The money had immediately turned her life from a downward spiral to a spike upward, sky high. She suddenly had the money to open a little bakery. Her dream-bubble had not been pricked after all. It was still intact.

Thoughts of the bakery and her to-do list charged into her head. Thank heaven for Mary Bloom, her grandmother. Without Gran, even with the money, Star didn't think she could pull off a new business.

She rolled over again onto her back. Umm, the sun feels good, soothing on my skin.

Tyler …

Star sat up, hugged her knees as she gazed out at the sparkling surf of the Atlantic Ocean. She missed him. How much she missed him had caught her off guard. The vacant spot he left in her thoughts was overwhelming. The minute he was gone she felt empty.

The bony cartoonist had captured her friendship the first day she stepped into the diner to apply for the job posted in the window. A close bond developed that never left her … his encouragement, help and, of course, his cartoons. Now he was in California, hired by an animation company with a contract from DreamWorks for a piece of a new animated film project.

Thinking of Tyler always brought a smile to her lips and a tug at her heart. Even though he promised to come back home for the holidays she wondered if he really could, if he really meant it, if …

Two tanned Tarzans, surfboards under their arms strolled by. One whistled at the pretty blonde in the blue and white polka-dot bikini sitting on the beach towel. He elbowed his friend to take a look. Grinning they darted into the water, began paddling out to find a wave.

Following in their wake, two children, holding kite strings tightly in their little hands, ran by, kicking up sand. Star smiled, *so many adventures lie ahead for those children* …

Refreshed, eager to start her own adventure, Star brushed the sand from her legs, punched her fists through the sleeves of the yellow shirt, folded the towel, and strutted up the beach to Atlantic Avenue to meet Gran. They had an appointment to sign the lease for her new business—Star's Bakery.

Chapter 1

HOT AND HUMID. Reaching the mid-eighties. That was the Daytona Beach forecast.

Star didn't give the weather a thought as she inserted the key into the lock. Hesitating, she grinned at Gran standing by her side, grinning in return. The pair knew the condition, the disrepair of the shop on the other side of the door, knew what equipment the previous baker had left. They had just signed the lease and it was now theirs to bring back to life.

"Ready, Gran? We know it's messy—"

"Filthy, dear," Gran interjected, her grin spreading ear to ear.

Star pushed open the back door and stepped into the kitchen.

Yes, it was grubby, but layers of baked on dough, fruit fillings and chocolate burned onto the stove top and oven walls, could be removed with elbow grease, some good old-fashioned scrubbing.

Before signing the lease she and Gran had tested the stove burners, tested the ovens, switched on the large double refrigerator leaving it running to be sure it cooled properly while they took measurements of the shop's floor space, the display cases, and windows.

The abandoned equipment worked—gas flames glowed brightly on the stove top, ovens reached a set temperature as did the fridge. The previous baker shut the doors one night skipping town, leaving everything in place including two display cases.

While the equipment worked it was sorely neglected giving the term stainless steel a bad rap.

The owner of the row of buildings on the short strip mall had received notice from the health department that an inspection would be required before the new renters could open for business.

As Star saw it, the equipment meant lots of hard labor but did not need to be replaced, at least not to begin with.

She had a little more than two months to transform the space into a sparkling, inviting bakery. That was the goal. The grand opening scheduled the Saturday before Thanksgiving ready to sell mouth-watering baked goods including a few European pastries to tease the eye as well as the palate. The goal was also to take orders for breads, pies, cakes and cookies for Thanksgiving and the following holidays.

Gran quickly stuck magnetic notepads to the refrigerator. To do lists—buy immediately, buy for the opening, buy for baking. Both women pulled on their oldest work clothes—Gran in frayed jeans, Star choosing shorts. Both wore sleeveless T-shirts, and old sneakers.

Star placed a cardboard box on the floor for their shoulder bags, and handed Gran a small headscarf. Both tied the daisy-covered scarves at the nape of their neck keeping hair out of their eyes and allowing air to circulate over their skin. Gran, no youngster when it came to cleaning, adjusted her scarf, a few silver waves with a diamond patch of black on the left side were left sticking out.

"I'll bring in the buckets and mops while you decide where you want to start," Star said wiping her hands on her shorts. Pausing, she hugged Gran, then strode out to her previously-owned red SUV. "Put a couple of table fans on the buy list," she called over her shoulder. "The AC doesn't seem very reliable. We'll need a breeze."

While the end of the summer heat had slipped to the mid-eighties, the mid-September temperature continued to rise along with the humidity.

Star and Gran worked feverishly, side by side, preparing for the opening of Star's Bakery in time for Thanksgiving. Morning, noon and evenings they spent bent over equipment scrubbing, polishing to new. Randomly calling out paint colors, wallpaper designs, furniture and décor ideas.

The most wonderful piece of luck happened a few days after they began the cleanup. Wanda and Charlie Armstrong appeared at the delivery door in back of the bakery. Refreshed from a two-week vacation and antsy for a new project, they asked Star if there was anything they could do to help.

Laughing with joy to see the former owners of the diner, Star hugged them both, grasped their hands pulling them into kitchen. Gran was in the midst of baking a pumpkin pie to test the oven she had just finished scouring. Seeing Wanda and Charlie, she too beamed with joy, hugging them, exclaiming how well they looked. Wanda happily received the hugs, glancing at the sad shape of the place, and said she could help out at least thirty hours a week. Charlie volunteered his services for a day or two here and there. The vacation had helped him to get back on his feet. His doctor said he could work but to be careful not to overdo. Charlie also offered the diner's van for hauling supplies. The backdoor still open, Gran and Star looked out at their red SUV parked next to the white van—*Charlie's Diner* painted on the side.

Charlie chuckled. "How about I replace Charlie's Diner with Star's Bakery? I know a guy who could have it a rolling billboard for your business in two days. Give me your phone number, and address, and if you have a picture—"

"Wait, wait. Charlie, I have just the thing." Star raced through the swinging door into the bakery shop, still grungy. She hadn't cleaned the shop except for one special spot. On the wall behind the counter was the framed cartoon Tyler drew the day before he left for California—a blonde baker girl smiling in front of a display case filled with cakes and cookies, lined on top with jars of taffy.

"Here," Star said holding out the frame to Charlie. "Do you think your sign man can transfer this somehow on the side of the van, and then maybe the door of our car?"

"I don't know but I'll find out," Charlie said taking the drawing from Star. Turning to leave, he called over his shoulder to Wanda. "I'm going to see what Teddy can do with this. Call if you need me. See you in a few."

Wanda strolled from the kitchen to the shop. Hands on her hips, she lifted a finger, running it over a thick layer of dust on the top of the glass case, swished the toe of her shoe on the floor. "Star, I need a bucket, sponges, and several bottles of heavy duty Mr. Clean. Unless you have something else with a higher priority, I'll tackle the shop." Wanda hightailed it out to the van, yelling at Charlie to stop. She returned with her work clothes including a small headscarf to keep her hair out of her eyes and off her neck. She was now one of the scullery maids.

Star hugged Gran, both wiping misty eyes. "Gran, can you believe this? We never admitted, didn't dare, that we wouldn't be ready to open in two months."

"Hey, you two, where's the bucket?"

"Wanda, we'll pay you as soon as—"

"Who said anything about money? I asked for a bucket and a mop if you have one. I'll make a list. Can I take that red love wagon out back—"

"We invested in the basic cleaning stuff when we tackled the kitchen. But, Wanda—"

"No *but Wanda*. Charlie and I turned a quick buck thanks to you and Tyler. We figure we owe you. Where is that boy? Still making his fortune in California?"

"About four weeks now. We text each other every day, sometimes more," Star said laughing, opening a water closet, pulling out a mop, bucket, and rags. "Anything you need, add to one of the lists on the fridge."

• • •

THE HEALTH INSPECTOR gave them the go-ahead to open, signing the document to be displayed near the back door. Gran took charge of the baked goods having cleaned the shelves, then stocking the ingredients. Star took charge setting up and decorating the shop, writing a press release to send to local news outlets—cable, radio stations, and the newspapers. Invitations were addressed ready to send to family and friends. Star's only family, other than Gran, was her mom and dad and two brothers in Hoboken, New Jersey.

While cleaning every square inch of the kitchen and shop alongside Wanda, Star took a break and bought four wrought-iron bistro tables with eight matching chairs. She positioned three inside along the wall. The fourth would be set outside every morning, beckoning passersby to stop for a coffee and pastry.

Time flew and suddenly only six days remained until the front door of Star's Bakery would open for the first time. The tempo of activity increased, reaching a high point along with frazzled nerves. Charlie hustled in the back door with four coffees. No one was in the kitchen, filled only with the delightful aroma of breads and cookies baking. Hitting the swinging door with his butt, he strode into the front. His wife was sitting at a little bistro table with Gran and Star. No one was talking. Very strange for three women, three very tired women. He put a large foam cup of coffee in front of each, pulled up a chair and sat.

Snapping back the spouts in the coffee lids, they took a long drink of the stimulus, sighed, then the chatter resumed in overdrive.

"We can wait on a bread slicer. Conserve our cash. Don't you think, Wanda?" Star asked glancing around. She smiled at Tyler's cartoon. The little baker girl was back in her place of honor, high on the wall behind the glass cases soon to be filled with pastries, cakes, and cookies.

Not bad. Not bad at all.

Chapter 2

Grand Opening
Star's Bakery

KA-CHING! KA-CHING!

The old cash register pinged merrily as Wanda tapped the keys. The Wurlitzer, along with the cash register from the diner, provided music of a different sort—the register ringing up sales, the Wurly playing Dolly Parton's rendition of *9 to 5*.

Star's vision of an old fashioned bakery transported customers back in time. Lace curtains loosely drawn to the side, held back with plaid ribbons tied in a bow, fringed the two picture windows.

Potted plants and bouquets of flowers from the Butterworth sisters, Benny, Tyler's mom and dad, and, of course, Liz, Manny, and Aunt Jane—all friends from the diner, wishing Star success in her new venture. A large bouquet of orange, red, and yellow mums in a cobalt-blue vase arrived from Star's family in Hoboken.

Star and Gran hoped that opening the week before Thanksgiving might entice holiday hosts and hostesses to visit the new little bakery and they were right. Many women looking for help with their big feast, kids in tow, stopped by to check out the shop on Atlantic Avenue. Pecan pie was a favorite—one less thing to worry about on their list.

Gran commandeered one of the bistro tables where she sat writing up orders like crazy. Pulling Star to the side, she whispered that she was concerned whether they would be able to fill all the orders—time, cash flow, helpers. Their heads together, they decided Gran should keep taking the orders. They'd fill them somehow. Meanwhile, Wanda pushed another rack of breads and pastries from the back to restock the glass cases.

As the sun set, Star turned on the little white lights lining the picture windows. She had sent a special invitation to the diner's most regular patrons as well as Tyler's parents inviting them to take a peek at her new shop. She and Gran expected their friends would drop by soon.

People stopping by after work to eyeball the new bakery were treated to complimentary coffee and Thanksgiving cupcakes—pumpkin, ginger spice, chocolate, and maple. All were frosted with butter cream icing.

It was a little after six o'clock, dusk, when Gran tapped Star's shoulder, pointing out the window. The Butterworth sisters had stopped out front, removing Benny's wheelchair from the trunk. Hattie and Mattie helped him navigate through the door while Anne parked around back.

Wanda started another brew cycle of the coffee maker, initially for fifty cups. The party urn was another hand-me down from the diner. Star had baked special cupcakes for the invited guests. A little pilgrim girl or boy, or turkey, guest's choice, were stuck into each cake placed on the counter next to the coffee setup.

It wasn't long before more special guests arrived following the Butterworth sisters and Benny, hugging their diner friends, joking, laughing—it was good to see each other again. When Liz saw the Wurly, she held out her hand to her husband. Manny filled her palm with five quarters. The little bakery was buzzing—ka-chings, Dolly Parton, and animated chatter.

Star, Gran, and Wanda were dressed in uniform—black leather flats, black hose, black skirt and white blouse with a ruffled white bib apron monogrammed in black cotton thread—
Star's Bakery.

Additional drop-ins mingled with the by-invitation group. Star spotted Benny off in the corner talking casually with a man she surmised was a businessman stopping by after work. He was dressed differently than the usual people along the Daytona Beach strip—a light-weight wool blazer tailored of a distinctive weave, gold emblem on the pocket Star didn't recognize. His black bow tie reminded her of Tyler, bringing a sudden tug to her heart.

Tyler's parents, Cindy and Tony Jackman, strolled in, giving Star and Gran a hug. Star caught them whispering in Gran's ear, the three exchanging devilish grins.

Star had made it a point to follow up on the invitation to the News Journal, asking if they could write an article on her grand opening. Maybe include a picture? Nothing more had been said so her eyes opened wide when not only a reporter but also a cameraman swept in and immediately began snapping photographs. The reporter spoke with Star who steered him to Gran and the special guests for background stories, as well as Benny and the man he was conversing with.

But nothing surprised Star as much as when Superman strolled into the shop.

Superman!

He was the real deal dressed in a red cape draped over a dark-blue, long-sleeve shirt, with a huge crimson *S* on a yellow diamond-shaped patch covering his chest. A yellow patent leather belt circled his waist, drawn through loops of the dark-blue trousers. The pant legs were caught inside knee-high red boots.

It was Tyler, her superman, standing with his hands on his hips. Running to him, Superman circled her with his muscular arms, twirling her in the air. Her shoes almost hit the man in the patterned wool blazer, walking with a wobbly gait through the merriment and out the door.

Tyler Jackman had bulked up. The red cape pulled back over his shoulders revealed biceps flexing like ticking time bombs when he strode around the little bakery hugging his former diner friends.

Private Eye, Liz Salinas, very pregnant, her baby due about Christmas, held out her hand and was rewarded with another handful of quarters from her husband to feed the Wurlitzer, keeping the Wurly rocking.

The News Journal team had their picture for the front page of the Sunday paper: *Superman visits new bakery on Atlantic Avenue.*

Chapter 3

WITH THE WURLY belting out another jazzy song, Superman embraced the new bakery's entrepreneur with a full-on press, dipping the smiling woman, snapping her up straight, dancing around the cases of cookies, cakes, and pies, finishing with an under-the-arm twirl. Laughing, they both bowed to their delighted audience.

It was then Tyler who was on the receiving end of the hugs. The Butterworth sisters jabbering like magpies at the change in Tyler. Black-rimmed glasses exchanged with contacts. At least that's what they thought. Surely, he still required help to see what he was drawing. But it was the muscles—where had they been hiding? His shock of dark brown hair was the same, a lock brushing his right eyebrow—definitely movie star handsome.

Star had enough of all the falderal fiddle de dee. Grasping Superman's hand, she drew him through the swinging doors to the kitchen. Gran immediately nudged over the bistro-order table blocking the entrance to the kitchen. Wanda, channeling Gran's move, stood next to her. No one was passing them, giving Superman and Star's reunion a little privacy.

Superman quickly enveloped the blue-eyed blonde in his arms, lowering his lips to her plump pink smile. With a quick hug, he stepped back, his eyes grazing over her head to toe.

"Miss Bloom, you look beautiful as ever," he said grinning.

"Well, Superman, you, on the other hand, *have* changed. No glasses, which, by the way, I found rather charming."

"Oh, then they will be back … what else?"

"You're taller, I'm sure."

"Not so, Miss Bloom. What else?"

"How did I ever miss those muscles, the shoulders, the washboard abs rippling under your shirt?"

"Ah, you noticed. The men in California, and the women looking them over, are obsessed with their physique. The small building the company is leasing has a gym and a coffee pot. A small counter-top refrigerator. We sign up for time slots in the gym to work out, tone up."

"But … in three months—"

Superman silenced her, wrapping his red cape around her, kissing her perky lips. With a sigh he released her, checked his watch. "Can you take me to Orlando? I have a flight back to Burbank in less than three hours. We should just be able to make it."

"How long have you been here?"

"Not quite five hours. Mom and Dad picked me up at the airport. We had an hour to swap stories, another hour or so for dinner. I swore them to secrecy but couldn't stop them from whispering to Gran when they saw her."

Star gaped at him. "You came all this way for my opening?"

"That's right, Miss Bloom. I borrowed the outfit from one of the studios. Do you like it?" Hands on his hips he turned around slowly ending with a peck on her forehead.

"You must be exhausted."

"Adrenalin. I couldn't sleep on the flight, but the return flight … let's just say I will have fond memories of your shocked face when I walked in the door."

"Okay. Let's get going. We can talk in the car. Speaking of car, wait until you see my traveling red billboard—a certain cartoon character painted on both sides."

"Hmm, a billboard. I have to say goodbye to Mom and Dad, then we can leave. They have my duffle bag. Is there a bathroom or a freezer I can change in?"

Giggling, Star stepped quickly to the catch-all water closet—supply shelves and restroom—nodding at the open door. She didn't know whether to laugh or cry. He was here, but he was leaving.

• • •

TYLER DROVE. Star's nerves were a jumble. Her reaction at seeing Superman was instantaneous, shocking him, flinging her arms around him. Now, she felt like she was going to hyperventilate as she peppered him with questions.

"What are the people like, the people you work with?"

"You'd love them. They're so excited about the project. We laugh a lot, showing our drawings to each other. We each have a piece and then at some point—hours, sometimes days, we put them together."

"Your day? I mean Southern California must be beautiful."

"When you grow up in Florida, you kind of expect the sun every day. The ocean is different. I can't explain it—beaches seem wider. There are high banks in places with mansions perched on top facing the ocean. You've seen news clips when pieces break off, sometimes the houses falling with the landslides. I took a drive up State Route 1 … exploring. We don't have banks like that in Florida, but the palm trees look the same."

"So you like the people you work with? Are they from California, or are they transplants like you?"

"Most of us are not from California—from all over the states. Like I said, we laugh a lot. Star, they're so talented. I'm learning so many tricks of the trade as they say."

"Girls? Pretty I bet."

Tyler smiled noting a tinge of jealousy? He reached for her hand, kissed her palm. Something that he heard from a co-worker makes a woman's blood run hot. "No one can hold a candle to you, Miss Bloom."

"Are you still planning on coming home for Christmas ... I mean this trip cost you ... and there will be parties out there, and—"

"Yes, Star. I'm definitely coming home. In fact, they're closing the project down from Christmas through New Year's day."

"Promise?"

"Promise!"

• • •

DRIVING, DEFLATED, Star fumbled for her cell lying on the passenger seat, tapped the numbers.

"Gran, I just dropped Tyler off and I'm heading home. I'm sorry I left you alone to close on our first day, but—"

"Nonsense. Don't you even think such a thing. You and Tyler had such a short time to see each other. Were you surprised he came to your opening?"

"Totally. Now he's gone again ... Gran, I'm having trouble with his leaving. I miss him already, but he promised me he'll still come home for Christmas."

"Star, with the orders I wrote up, I'm thinking that after the Thanksgiving rush we should move. You know, get a place with walls."

Laughing, Star replied. "What, you don't like my one room studio, your mattress bed, and me on the futon? Yes, Gran, I think we've earned some walls. But let's wait until after the holidays. Cash is a bit tight right now."

Star said goodbye and burst into tears. "What's wrong with me?" she whispered to the woman in the rearview mirror. Tugging at her apron, loosening it enough to reach her eyes, she wiped away the tears, but they kept coming. Then she began to hiccup. She laughed. More hiccups, more tears. "Good thing Tyler's not here, missy, he'd go crazy drawing a cartoon of the little baker girl, big tears rolling down her face." She laughed harder thinking of him and his cartoons which brought on another bout of hiccups and tears.

Chapter 4

AT 10:42 P.M. Detective Fred Watson, Daytona Beach Police Department, was about to turn off his computer for the day when he received a call from the morgue. A John Doe, age sixty-five to seventy-five, was found dead near the Daytona Beach Ferris wheel.

A foot patrolman and his partner found the body. Their initial assessment—the man died of a heart attack. However, he was picked clean—no wallet, no jewelry. Clothing was worn but of high quality, very expensive.

"No identification? No name?" Watson asked.

"That's right." The morgue technician was hoping for a quiet night. "What do you want us to do?"

"So, the patrolman thought heart attack. What's your assessment on how he died? Any foul play? Wounds? Drugs?"

"No wounds. I can't tell about the drugs unless we pump his stomach, order a workup on his blood."

"Okay. Go ahead with the usual routine—blood and stomach. I'll be over at ... when do you think you'll have the results?"

"Depends on the lab. This time of night, well, maybe by early morning, four."

"I want to see the clothes. Bag them. Are you still on at 5:30?"

"Yup. Here till six."

. . .

STAR TOSSED AND TURNED, glanced at the clock glowing on the floor beside the futon-couch—2:32 a.m. *Tyler should be in California.* She sighed, a long puff of air over her lips. *The grand opening was a big success.* She thought of Superman. Once again Ty had raised the event, punching up the excitement. She glanced over at Gran, heard her rhythmic breathing.

Her eyes misted with the visions of everything Gran had done for her over the last few months ... and particularly the opening— sitting at the little table, carefully writing up the orders, fearful she was going to transpose a digit on a telephone number. An enormous wave of love flooded through Star. Her Gran was so special.

Ping!

Star grabbed for her cell.

A text from Ty.

• • •

"Just landed. Waiting in line to exit plane. U R home safe? T."

Sitting up on the futon she typed a reply. "I safe. Thank U. Car? S."

"Yah. Clunker. Luv CA but Luv FL more. U a big success. Gran too. She OK if I call her Gran? Sleep tight. T."

"*Gran* would love it. More tomorrow. S."

Chapter 5

AT 6:30 A.M. Detective Watson called Manny Salinas, private investigator, retired department chief from the DBPD, Daytona Beach Police Department, still on call when extra help was needed. "Good morning, Manny. Trust I didn't get you up." Watson chuckled to himself. Once a cop always a cop and early rising is part of a cop's DNA.

"No, Fred, you didn't wake me up. Liz and I were just enjoying our first cup of coffee, watching the morning news. And, good morning to you. What's up?"

"A guy was found by the Ferris wheel last night, Daytona Beach. No ID. I was wondering if you could give us a hand? We had a rash of accidents … I know it's not big time, but it sure would help us out, if you could—"

Manny put his hand over the mouthpiece of the cordless phone, and whispered to his wife. "Want to join me on an ID caper this morning?"

Liz, a private investigator with her husband, nodded yes, stretched, yawned, slumped back in the chair. A little less than a month until their baby was due, she needed a good excuse to move out of the chair. Even the sparks from the ringlets in her red hair seemed to fizzle.

"I think we can accommodate you, Detective," Manny said mimicking Fred's chuckle. "What do you have so far? Is John Doe at the morgue?"

"Yes, and there's practically nothing to go on. I think someone stole his wallet and any jewelry he might have been wearing. However, they didn't strip the poor guy of his clothes."

"Did you order a lab work-up on him?"

"Yeah. The results should be available within the hour. When do you think you can swing by?"

Manny raised his brows to Liz—*time*?

Liz looked at her watch. Oh God, she was going to have to move out of the comfy chair. "Eight-thirty, nine?"

"Did you hear that, Fred?"

"Yup. I'll tell the coroner. Let me know what you think after you see him. Keep me posted."

"I will. Shoot 'em straight."

Fred laughed. He had missed the leg of a perp once. The thug got away and Manny was never going to let him forget it.

Manny laughed with the detective and disconnected the call. He pulled Liz up out of her chair, held her in his arms, allowing room for the ever-growing baby bump. "You're sure you want to come with me?"

"Yes. The waiting for the big reveal is getting to me. A nice simple John Doe investigation could be just what the doctor ordered to get me moving."

Chapter 6

THE DIGITAL CLOCK displayed 8:30 a.m. The early Sunday morning sun, playing hide-and-seek with the clouds, suddenly streamed in the front picture windows of Star's Bakery. The burst of sunlight through the lace tieback curtains painted a filigree pattern across the white tiled floor.

Star and Gran stood at the cash register. How could one day be so different than the day before—chaos, excitement, and then eerie silence? Even the temperature—hot hitting ninety then, now a cool seventy-nine, sunny to cloudy with a prediction of rain to come.

Friday they were scrambling in preparation for the grand opening the next day. Saturday was a blur. No time to think only to act.

The opening had been a huge success. Seeing all their friends, their smiles, their words of encouragement and support, snapping up several items before they left, was thrilling. The little cash register ka-chinging, Gran taking orders. Two high school girls hired to help, had rummaged in their closets to mimic the bakery uniform—short black skirt, white blouse, black bib apron—were the epitome of customer service. All smiles, thanking each patron for the sale.

After much discussion on which day would be the best to open, Gran and Wanda agreed with Star that a Saturday would be preferable. People would have more time to drop by. Star and

Gran would have time the next day, Sunday being closed, to replenish the stock and fix any glitches that occurred during the opening.

Star glanced at her grandmother, both were back in their comfy clothes—capris, T-shirts, sandals. "Were we dreaming, or did we just about sell out?"

"You're not dreaming, dear. My fingers feel a bit cramped from holding the pen so tight writing up orders."

Hearing the back door bang shut, they both looked up to see Wanda striding from the kitchen, through the swinging doors to the shop. She was juggling two loose-leaf binders, a shoulder bag, cardboard tray with three Starbucks' coffees.

"Okay, you two, we have some serious business to attend to." Setting the coffee on the table that served as the order station for Gran the day before, Wanda dropped the binders alongside the coffee, pulled up two more chairs and sat down. Brows raised, she nodded for Star and Gran to sit.

Star's brows squeezed together. What could possibly be bothering Wanda?

"The good news is that yesterday was a big success and, by my calculations, we even managed to eke out a profit."

"Wanda, that's wonderful. And, thanks for the coffee." Star passed out the foam coffees, along with sugar packets and little creamer cups. Tossing the tray in the trash, she looked at Wanda waiting for the "but" word.

"But, after looking at the orders Mary wrote up, at the *very successful* opening, we are headed for trouble."

"What trouble is that?" Gran asked taking a sip of coffee. "Umm, I needed this. How about you, dear?"

Star nodded, staring wide-eyed at Wanda, who also chose comfort with jeans and a T-shirt. "What trouble?"

"Cash flow trouble. We have bills to pay—setting up the bakery, equipment, and then the supplies. The bank balance … to be kind, let's just call it way too low. Yesterday we made a profit, thank heavens, but going forward we have to watch every penny or you'll be closing before you know it."

"Do we have enough to cover the orders I wrote up yesterday?" Gran asked.

"Yes, but there isn't much left. Then comes Christmas, and parties, other holidays. You won't catch a break on expenses until after the first of the year. It'll be touch and go. If the customers pay on receipt for their Thanksgiving orders, which they should, that will help. Of course, the bad news is after the holidays the orders will trail off. Then we have to make it on daily traffic … hopefully a steady flow of daily traffic."

"Wanda, can we survive?" Star slumped back in the wrought-iron bistro chair.

"I think so. Barely. I'll monitor the expenses and run the daily receipts to the bank immediately after we close. So, ladies, let's get cracking on those orders. Write up your lists for ingredients, supplies."

"The white boxes and bags for cakes and cookies—there should be enough for the orders," Star said. "If we run out of the ones printed with Ty's little baker girl and the name of the shop, we'll have to make-do with plain white. Wait until after the holidays, check our finances before we order more."

"I disagree," Wanda countered. "Hon, if you're running low, let me know. Marketing is key, and a reminder to customers where the goodies came from when they carry out their purchases. Your logo and name is not a place to scrimp. The newspaper story, I'm sure they'll run it … in fact, let's take a look. I bought a copy when I picked up the coffee." Wanda opened the newspaper, laying it on top of the binders.

"Oh, my. Look, Gran. Superman's bowing to a customer holding a bag of cookies." Star looked up at Wanda, hope written across her face. *The newspaper story should help bring in business. They had to be ready to fill the orders for Thanksgiving in four days.*

"Star dear, we can't move yet."

"But, Gran, you can't sleep any longer on that—"

"I saw some bunk beds in the consignment shop down the street. That will get you off the futon and me off the mattress. Don't you think?"

"Yes, Gran. I think."

A shard of light bounced off the old Wurlitzer's glass hitting Star in the eye. Grinning, she stepped quickly to the Wurly retrieving the coins from yesterday's opening. "Would you look at this?" Grabbing a white cookie bag, she dumped in the coins. "Must be more than fifty." Returning to the player she stuffed several coins in the slots punching selections. With Dolly Parton belting *9 to 5* from the movie soundtrack, filling the shop with the catchy tune, Star returned to the table. "Okay, Gran, we'll buy the bunk beds. Now, let's get going on our to-do lists for Wanda."

● ● ●

"Hi, Ty. Money tight. U thoughts on selling Gran's taffy online? S."

...

"I'll start bakery website. Fine tune it at Xmas. Miss you. T."

Chapter 7

MANNY AND LIZ sat across the desk from the Daytona Beach Medical Examiner. Both PIs were dressed head to toe in black—their uniform. Liz thought her look quite stylish given her condition—black maternity trousers and a shirt with the dimensions of a pup tent.

The ME and Manny were old friends. Liz was more of a casual acquaintance having met with him three times in her capacity as a private investigator.

The Medical Examiner filled them in on what was known about John Doe, precious little, adding nothing more than what Detective Watson had told Manny over the phone. Time of death was determined to have been within an hour or two of when he was found by the patrolmen given the body's state of rigor mortis.

"Detective Watson asked us to try to identify the man," Manny said leaning forward, right hand fingering his moustache.

"Yes, he told me."

"Can we see the body?" Liz asked rubbing a muscle in her lower back.

"And, we need to take a picture," Manny added. "We also want to examine what he was wearing and anything else you found on him."

"Sure, come with me. The lab report on his blood, contents of his stomach, hasn't shown up yet. There were several fatal accidents last night and a shooting at a bar. I guess that's why Watson called you. An autopsy hasn't been ordered. I'll let you know when I get the lab report."

The private investigators followed the ME into the refrigerated vault—icy cold with a heavy odor of bleach. He pulled open the slot holding John Doe. Liz, her face scrunched in distaste, took a picture of the man, a close up of his head.

Back in the examiner's office they checked the container holding what John Doe last had on his person.

"Wow! Very expensive clothes. Look at this, Manny," Liz said showing him the label on the blazer. "Yohji Yamamoto. Have you heard of him?"

"Can't say as I have. Who is he? That jacket is something else." Manny fingered the soft, silky fabric as Liz snapped several pictures of the clothing.

"He, my dear husband, is a world-famous Japanese designer. Let me read you this label. 'Khaki, navy and burgundy foulard-print cotton and linen blend.' As you can see, it's a classy single-breasted, three-button blazer."

"And you know all this because?"

Liz sighed, shook her head in disbelief, then smiled. "I had a case, Japanese man. He wore a jacket similar to this. Foulard is a French word. A foulard fabric is usually a small printed design of various colors—handkerchiefs and neckties are made from this fabric. It's a small-scale, tailored pattern with a basic block repeat."

"While it's not my cup of tea, the small diamond pattern has, as you said, a tailored look. How much are you talking for a jacket like this? Do you have that in your pretty head?" Manny glanced at Liz grinning back at him.

"Oh ... about two grand."

Manny whistled. "Two-thousand dollars?"

"Plus or minus a few hundred. Look, there's a name sewn in the lining. Thomas Elliott." Liz held the jacket open so Manny could see the name, and then snapped another picture. "We're good, partner. We may have solved the case before we started." Liz giggled along with a light smack on his cheek.

The ME sat at his desk leafing through a few sheets of paper. "Heard you talking. Thomas Elliott? We missed that. As I said, it was a hectic night. With no wallet for a quick ID, they must have thrown his clothes in a bin and then went on to one of the accident fatalities. I did a search in the state's telephone database while you took the pictures. There were several Elliotts. Here's a printout of what I found. Phone numbers but no ages. You may have an easy one here … except for notifying his family, if he has a family."

"How old would you say John Doe was?" Manny asked.

"It's hard to tell. Weathered skin, but not overly so. Hair a light gray but not silver. Heck, Manny, I don't know. Could be anywhere from mid-sixties to late seventies. You saw him. Where would you put him?"

"Your guess is as good as mine. Okay, we'll keep you posted. The officers who found him … I'll give them a jingle. Talk to them. Visit where they found the body. Stitch, I'll take you back to the office so you can start trying to find this Thomas Elliott."

"Ahh, offices. Big time private eyes," the examiner said with a chuckle.

"Two offices … adjoining," Liz said, smiling sweetly as she glanced up at her lifetime partner. She got a kick when he used the nickname he gave her, calling her Stitch when they were working a case.

"Home offices," Manny said. "Come on, Stitch, we have work to do."

Chapter 8

WALKING OUT OF the sterile morgue to the car, Liz shot a pensive look at her husband. "Not much at home for breakfast, or, I guess it's lunchtime. I'm really hungry, Manny."

Manny held the car door for her. Satisfied that his wife was settled with her seatbelt, he slid in behind the wheel.

"Luckily we have a loaf of sour dough bread from Star's Bakery … that was fun yesterday wasn't it?"

"Sure was. Star and her grandmother looked so happy. They worked hard cleaning up the place, getting it ready for the opening. I saw it just after they signed the lease—great location on Atlantic Avenue, nice cozy size, but it needed some serious scouring. It was a bakery before. Did you know that?"

"No, I didn't. So the display cases were already there?"

"Yup. Manny, I hope she can make a go of it. That hundred thousand won't last long. Funny how things work out—Wanda working with them as office manager. I guess that's what she's doing. Having run the diner, she'll be a huge help on the business end."

"When we get home, you take a little nap while I fix us some sandwiches."

"Okay, then we split up the list Fred gave us. What if John Doe, maybe Thomas Elliott from the name embroidered in the jacket, was just passing through? Not from Florida?" Liz asked glancing at her husband.

"First things first. Nap, then the list. At least we have a place to start."

• • •

REFRESHED FROM HER NAP, Liz joined Manny in the kitchen. Over a sandwich of ham and cheese on sour dough bread, dill pickles for Liz, mustard on both, they split up the list of names, one-hundred-seven in all.

Sitting at their desks in adjoining offices, they both started punching in the numbers. Liz had fifty names, the balance were on the two sheets of paper in front of Manny.

Thirty minutes passed. "Any luck, Stitch?"

"No. Everyone present and accounted for so far. Glad it's Sunday, I only had one call go to voicemail."

"Coffee?"

"I think tea, thanks."

Standing, rubbing her back, Liz sat back down, and punched the next number.

"Hello."

"Hi, I'm a private investigator in Daytona Beach. I'm looking for a Thomas Elliott. I was given your number. By any chance is Mr. Elliott there?" Liz leaned back, laid her pen down, rubbed her lower back.

"I'm sorry, he's out. I'm Mrs. Elliott. Is there something I can help you with?"

"Mrs. Elliott, my name is Elizabeth Stitchway. I'm looking for a Thomas Elliott who owns a very distinctive blazer, a Yohji Yamamoto design."

Liz could hear Mrs. Elliott laugh. "Oh, my, for a minute I thought something had happened to my husband. He's away on business. But to answer your question, my husband used to invest in Yamamoto menswear. He felt he had to play the part."

"Excuse me, play the part?"

"Yes, Tom is a developer here in Miami. Actually up the west side of the state to Tampa, and up the east coast to Fort Lauderdale, and points in between."

"Could you describe your husband for me, Mrs. Elliott—you know height, weight, hair and eye color?"

"Now, you're scaring me again."

"No, no, I'm sure everything is okay. The description please?"

"Well he's fifty-two, tall—about six-one. Blue eyes, and sandy hair. Turning gray much to his chagrin."

"Mrs. Elliott, you said your husband used to wear Yamamoto clothing. Any chance he still has a blazer?"

"Oh, no. All his Yamamoto went to Goodwill. I don't know where. Our housekeeper lived in Orlando ... maybe—"

"Can you give me her name?"

"Kathy Dalton."

"Does she still work for you?"

"No. She moved to be near her children. Atlanta I think. Wait, she sent me a postcard. I have her address. Sorry, no telephone number."

Liz covered her phone's mouthpiece. "Manny, Manny, come here."

"Ms. Stitchway, are you still there?"

"Yes, yes, go ahead." Liz wrote the address on her legal-size pad of paper, read it back to Mrs. Elliott. "Thank you, Mrs. Elliott. You've been most helpful."

"Ms. Stitchway, can you tell me why you're looking for Tom?"

"A body was found in Daytona Beach last night, near the Ferris wheel next to the boardwalk. We're trying to identify the man. The only clue we have is that Thomas Elliott was embroidered in his jacket, a Yamamoto blazer. From the description you gave me of your husband, John Doe doesn't match up. I'm sure John Doe is not your husband. If you have any information you think might be helpful, I'd appreciate your calling me."

"Well, it could have been Tom's blazer. He liked to have his name somewhere on his clothes. Yamamoto is an expensive designer. Can you tell me the colors of the design?"

"Yes—khaki, burgundy, and navy."

"Sure sounds like Tom's blazer all right."

Liz gave Mrs. Elliott her cell number, said goodbye, and disconnected the call. Sipping her tea, she sat grinning up at Manny as she handed him her notes on the yellow pad.

Taking back her notes, hitting Manny's arm with the pad, Liz called information. The automated service gave her two numbers. One, a K. Dalton, the other a T. Dalton. Liz struck pay dirt with the first one. K. Dalton turned out to be a pleasant older lady who had worked for the Elliotts, and, yes, she remembered Mr. Elliott's blazer. "Who could forget that jacket?" she quipped. Within a week after Mrs. Elliott had given her a bundle of clothes for Goodwill, K. Dalton dropped the lot off at Goodwill in Orlando, Curry Ford Road, around November of last year.

Liz did a quick internet search for a Goodwill, Orlando, Curry Ford Road. With an eye on her monitor, she punched in the number, asked for the manager. At first the manager tried to brush her off, but when Liz said she was a private investigator the woman was more cooperative, scanning her records for November of the prior year.

"Oh, yes. The Yamamoto blazer. Actually, I handled the sale. I remember because we were surprised—the other women and I. We were on duty together. The jacket was priced at fifty dollars. The man gave me five hundred. Very unusual. But things happen—donation to a charity."

A grin spread on Liz's face as she glanced from Manny to her notepad, underlining fifty and five hundred.

"Sorry, the customer's name was not written in the journal."

The grin turned to a frown after she said goodbye to Goodwill Orlando.

"Manny, darn it all, the jacket was a cash sale. But how could John Doe afford it? He didn't look like he had that kind of money except his hands were smooth. He was not a laborer."

"You did good, Stitch. But it looks like we hit a dead end."

Chapter 9

IT WAS MONDAY MORNING. Manny was in the kitchen trying not to wake Liz. Their pooches—Peaches, a black Lab mix, and Maggie, a Border collie mix, rescue dogs—were outside for their morning constitution and suddenly began barking. They had treed a cat. Inadvertently, they had also roused their mistress.

Stretching, yawning, Liz padded into the kitchen, easing up on a stool at the island counter. Manny was ready with her coffee. Kissing her on the forehead under a wayward cluster of red curls, he retrieved his cell phone from his belt. Glancing at the display, he answered. "Detective Fred Watson, good morning to you."

"You're in a chipper mood, Manny."

"Always, Detective. What can I do for you?"

"The John Doe lab report just came in."

"And."

"And, we may have a murder on our hands. Remnants in his stomach showed what he had last ingested—steak, pumpkin of some kind, and arsenic."

"Oh, oh."

"Yeah, and his blood had a fairly high level of a barbiturate, like an antidepressant. He could have overdosed but with the arsenic … I don't know. Being a John Doe we haven't performed an autopsy. I'd like to hold off until he can be ID'd. Any luck on your end?"

"Yes and no. Liz traced the jacket to the name sewn inside—Thomas Elliott. Mr. Elliott was out of town, but the misses said the jacket had been given to a housekeeper, who in turn dropped it off at an Orlando Goodwill. It was purchased in a period of days, last November, by a man who paid cash. Lots of cash. The jacket was priced at fifty dollars and the man paid five hundred telling the woman to keep the change. As I said … yes, we traced the jacket but then hit a dead end."

"The routine police report will show up in today's paper—John Doe, date and time the body was found, and location. We'll run it again and add a line asking the public for help, if anyone has information about John Doe to call the DBPD. I'll include a description of him—approximate age, hair, and definitely the jacket."

"Okay. Let me know if you get any tips. Liz and I will follow up."

"Thanks, Manny. You wouldn't believe how chaotic it is around here. Well, I guess you would know, retired captain that you are. Maybe I should try for early retirement."

Chapter 10

BENNY LOVED HOW his life was changing—a loner with no friends, then Charlie's Diner where he started having his morning coffee, and now at Star's Bakery. He missed the funny cartoon man, Tyler, but his favorite friend was Star. She never ceased to amaze him.

Benny was orphaned as a baby, passed from one foster home to another. He never knew the details of his birth, never questioned or searched for answers. He was a good boy but withdrawn. The last three foster homes treated him kindly but when he completed high school he joined a traveling circus, said goodbye to his foster parents and never looked back.

He performed whatever jobs the circus needed and, under the tutelage of the circus production manager, learned the tricks of the trade. A quick minded, strong lad, he soon became the production manager's assistant. As years went by the circus became out of favor. However, the circus Benny was attached to was one of the few that survived, for awhile anyway.

To attract an audience, high-wire acts became more and more daring. Benny, while strong, was slim of frame. Whenever the star of the show trained, whenever she performed, Benny could always be found watching the beautiful Mademoiselle Gigi through loving eyes. Gigi could feel his eyes on her, the eyes of a handsome man. He was different than the rest of the men in the circus who used trickery to get her alone in her trailer. One day

Mademoiselle Gigi asked Benny if he would like to try the high wire. He asked his boss if he could train on the wire. He was granted permission so long as the time he spent with Gigi didn't interfere with his duties.

Benny was fearless, daring, pushing himself from simple tricks to more complex, from using a net to demanding it be removed. The boss liked the act. The audience held their breath as the young man dared ever riskier movements.

His fate was sealed one night, a final performance on the fairgrounds in Jacksonville, Florida. It was a hot night, humidity soared, the crowd large looking for a diversion under the big tent where the trapeze acts performed. Benny fell that night rendering him partially paralyzed. He became wheelchair bound, only able to stand briefly to swing, pivot his body from a kitchen chair to his wheelchair, to move from the wheelchair to a chair in the shower.

Now fifty-nine, Benny managed to make ends meet by living simply on disability insurance. His big splurge was breakfast at the diner on Atlantic Avenue, a couple of blocks down the street. With the aid of his motorized wheelchair he could indulge in this trip.

On any given morning he could be spotted wearing a short-sleeved plaid shirt held tight with red suspenders, his thick salt and pepper hair grazing his shoulders touching tufts of gray hair on his chin. His muscular arms, attesting to workouts at home with a set of free weights, were a sharp contrast to the skinny legs that dropped to the foot supports. No matter the wheelchair, Benny had a sweet smile that included a twinkle in his pale gray eyes.

With talk of the diner closing, he became fearful of losing contact with his diner friends—the Butterworth sisters, the funny waiter Tyler who drew cartoons of him and his confounded wheelchair, and, of course, Star. What was he going to do?

Star told him not to worry. That when the diner closed she planned to open a little bakery —only two blocks further up from the diner on Atlantic Avenue. The bakery would have a few small round tables so Benny could have his coffee and a pastry, reunite with some of his diner friends. Not only that, but she invited him to a pre-opening, a test of sorts.

Two days before the opening, Wanda had to run to the store for some supplies. A sign in the window invited potential customers to visit the bakery from nine to eleven before the Grand Opening. Star was helping a drop-in, then another. A customer stood at the register tapping her foot, looking for Star to ring up her sale. Benny wheeled up to the cash register, stood clutching the edge of the counter and rang-up the cranky customer. There was nothing wrong with Benny's mind, arms, or fingers. When he saw a job that had to be done he did it.

Star caught the transaction out of the corner of her eye.

She talked to Wanda when she returned with the supplies, told her what had transpired. In return, the two women conspired to give Benny a try. Maybe offer him a job. If he could handle the register for a couple of hours, a couple of times a week, he could earn free coffee, a cookie, a loaf of bread—whatever he could carry in the pouch on the back of his wheelchair. The bakery wasn't in a financial position to hire anybody, not now, but maybe in the future.

The Monday after the opening Benny became a permanent fixture at Star's Bakery.

Leaving his room, ground floor studio he called it, he began a routine, motoring along the sidewalk on Atlantic Avenue nodding to passersby. Stopping at the News Journal box, he pushed the coins in the slot, folded the newspaper tucking it in his chair, and rolled to the front door of the bakery. Star was waiting for him.

He rolled up to the coffee service, poured a cup adding a dash of sugar and a mini container of cream, then rolled to the bistro table to read the paper.

At the stroke of 9:00 a.m. he would be ready to take over the cash register—swing up to a higher chair Star purchased just for him, perfect to give the register a work out. Turning the page of the newspaper, he took another sip of coffee. Yup, this was going to be a dandy way to start his day.

Ka-ching!

Chapter 11

BENNY WAS ENJOYING his coffee, reading the newspaper, before beginning his day on the job. "Star, did you see the article in today's paper? The police reports? Third one down. Seems a man's body was found by the Ferris wheel Saturday night, late. No identification. Calling him John Doe."

Star was adding fresh-baked cookies, arranged on a red pottery plate, to the display case. "What caught your eye, Benny?"

"His description. His clothes. There is a very detailed account of his jacket."

"Yeah?"

"Yeah. I wonder if John Doe is the man I talked to at your opening. Sure sounds like him … his jacket. I could tell it was expensive. The article ends with a telephone number. Do you think I should call?"

"Here's my cell, Benny. Go for it. I have to bring a couple of cakes out."

Benny took Star's cell. He could have used his own but it was in a zippered pouch—much easier to place a quick call with Star's phone.

"Daytona Beach Police Department. Can I help you?"

"I'm calling about John Doe, the man you found Saturday by the Ferris wheel."

"Your name, please?"

"Benny Howard."

"Do you have information, sir?"

"Well, I don't know if I do. Probably not. But the jacket description—"

"One moment, sir. I'll transfer you to Detective Watson."

Benny chuckled while he waited for the detective to pick up. *Small world,* he thought. He had met the detective, at least if it was the same Watson, a few months back. A Detective Watson had interviewed him about a robbery at the diner.

"Detective Watson."

"Hi, you probably don't remember me ... well maybe you do ... name is Benny. You questioned me at the diner robbery. I'm the guy in the wheelchair." Benny chuckled. *Dang chair was good for something.*

"Sure, I remember you, Benny. So, you think you might be able to identify John Doe?"

"I don't know ... but the jacket sounds very unusual."

"If we picked you up, do you think you could come down to the morgue, take a look to see if it's the man you ... exactly how do you know John Doe?"

"Saturday night. Star's Bakery opening. I wouldn't go so far as to say I know him, but there was this man. He and I chatted for at least a half an hour."

"Did he give you his name?"

"Sorry, Detective. We didn't exchange names."

"Okay, well an officer will pick you up, say in an hour? Where will you be?"

"That would work. I'll be at Star's Bakery, Atlantic Avenue. I'm the cashier." Benny grinned. Wow, he had a title.

● ● ●

"STAR, I HAVE TO RUN an errand but I'll be back."

"Anything I can get for you?"

Benny grinned. "Nah, it's police business. Official police business."

They both looked up as Manny and Liz strolled into the bakery. Star and Liz hugged leaving Manny to grin at Benny as they shook hands.

"Come on, Liz. There will be time for hugs later. We're here on police business. We've been tasked with picking up one Benny Howard. Escort Mr. Howard to the morgue."

Star looked bug-eyed at Benny. "You didn't tell me they want you to go to the morgue."

"Well, as Tyler would say, 'Miss Bloom, I'm just following orders.'"

"Hold on you two," Star said, yanking off her apron. "Benny goes, I go. Just let me tell Wanda. I'll be right with you."

"Okay," Manny said as Liz linked her arm through his. "So, Benny, you think you can identify this John Doe guy?"

"Maybe, yes. Maybe, no."

Settling Benny in the front seat of the black SUV, which wasn't all that easy given the height of the first step, Manny stashed the wheelchair in the back as Liz and Star climbed into the backseat. Waving to Wanda, the trio disappeared down the street, chauffeured by a retired police captain.

Detective Watson met them at the front door of the morgue, escorting the group to the refrigerated vault. Watson was a formidable figure. The six-foot black man came from Santa Fe, New Mexico, where he worked in law enforcement as a border guard. His muscular, burly body was intimidating. A scar across his left cheek spoke clearly that not all were intimidated.

Identification of John Doe was quick.

"Yup, that's the guy," Benny said, grim faced, shuddering at the sight of the body.

Star stepped back, looked the other way. She had never seen a dead person like that, face drained of color.

The lab tech slid the body back into the vault. Watson asked the group to follow him to a small conference room. He had a few questions for Benny. On the way he asked Star if she recognized John Doe. She shook her head. She had been totally occupied with Superman.

Watson laid a recorder on the conference room table. "Okay, Mr. Howard—"

"Can we keep it to Benny, Detective?"

"Sure, Benny. Tell me everything you remember about when, what time exactly, how, what the man said to you Saturday night."

"Whew. Let's see. Not much to say really. I was chatting on and on about Star, about how great she is getting the bakery going. Oh, and about her grandmother. Her name is Mary Bloom. As I said, chatting with him, small talk. You know, being polite."

"Name?" Watson asked.

"Sorry, Detective. Like I said on the phone, we never exchanged names. I guess I did most of the talking. Come to think of it, he didn't say much of anything. I did ask him where he was from."

"What did he say," Watson asked.

"Texas. Oil fields of Texas. That was it. Ate a pumpkin cupcake and left. Like I said, I did all the talking."

• • •

WATSON CLOSED THE FILE FOLDER. John Doe's death was not adding up no matter how he figured it. The man bought an expensive designer jacket at Goodwill priced at fifty dollars but paid five hundred. Of course, there could have been another owner in between Goodwill and John Doe, but for now he'd stick with what he had.

The lab report showed he had a significant amount of barbiturates in his stomach along with pumpkin, and the kicker— arsenic. The word arsenic jumped out of the screen at him—rat poison, an over-the-counter killer.

It was clear the case called for two actions. Watson hated to do it, but he couldn't play favorites with a potential murder. First, given Benny talked to Doe at the bakery, and the man had pumpkin in his stomach along with the arsenic, he had to dispatch an officer out to the bakery, unannounced, to shut it down while they searched the premises for rat poison. He couldn't fathom any reason why a person at the bakery would feed John Doe poison, but he had to check the possibility off his list.

The second course of action was to contact his counterpart in Dallas, Texas. The only clue that Benny could remember—Doe said he was from, lived, or at least worked in Texas.

Watson called Dallas PD, told the operator he wanted to be connected to a detective. He had a John Doe and there was a chance he was from Dallas, or, heaven forbid, somewhere else in the vast state of Texas.

The Dallas detective came on the line, asked Watson to send a picture and a description of the John Doe as well as his rather unusual clothing. He would see that the item was included in the next police department article, run it for a few days in all the major newspapers—Dallas, Houston, Austin, to name a few.

Chapter 12

THE DRIVE BACK to the bakery was a double Q—Quick and Quiet. Benny staring out one window, Star the other. Liz exchanged a glance or two with Manny.

They all trooped inside. Star pushing Benny's chair, Liz holding the door open. Manny bought a loaf of rye bread, and Liz decided to pamper her sweet tooth with a half-dozen cupcakes. Saying goodbye to Star, Manny paid the cashier for the items, exchanging grins with Benny. With their purchases on the backseat, Manny pulled out of the parking lot, spotting a black and white pulling to the curb parking in front of the bakery.

Inside the bakery, Benny was surprised to see two officers walk in the door. He remained at his post at the cash register.

Star smiled at the officers. "Hi, something I can package up for you two?" Star asked.

The first officer showed Star his badge as the second officer strode past Benny, walking straight through the swinging doors, disappearing in the back.

"Officer Trippy, Miss. Your name?" Trippy asked pocketing his badge.

"Star Bloom. This is my bakery. Is something wrong?"

The officer glanced at Benny squinting back at him. "Are you Mr. Howard?" Trippy asked.

"Yes, sir."

Turning his gaze back to Star, Trippy said, "I'm sorry to inconvenience you, Ms. Bloom, but I have to ask you to close the shop while we conduct a search of your bakery. Do you have a *We are closed* sign or something like that?"

"Come on, Officer. What's this all about?"

"A routine search. Probably nothing to be alarmed about. Seems Mr. Howard talked to a man we found Saturday night—"

"We were just at the morgue. Benny identified the body as the man he talked to at the opening of the bakery. So you know the man was here. What are you looking for? We really can't close the bakery. We're in the process of baking, of trying to fill the orders for Thanksgiving. Officer, I can't spare a minute, let alone an hour, let alone closing the shop."

"The sooner we can look around the sooner we'll be out of your hair. Is there anyone in the back?"

"Yes, Wanda Armstrong, my office manager. Actually she does most everything, and my grandmother. As I said we're trying to fill the orders. I'm sure you can smell the bread baking. Now, tell me what you're looking for."

"Do you have any rat poison, roach bait, or anything like that for pests?"

"Heavens no. Why would I—"

The officer who had breezed through the swinging doors to the kitchen returned, Gran sputtering behind him that she personally had purchased the bait. She'd never seen any critters, and she wanted to make sure it stayed that way. She added that a local company had come to spray twice while she and her granddaughter were cleaning, and why was the officer looking for roach hotels anyway. "This is all so upsetting."

The officer held a box labeled, *Twelve Roach Hotels. Guaranteed to stop roaches and ants in their tracks.* Bagging the box of hotels, he quickly finished up the search of the shop while Gran continued protesting.

Star looked at the officers in disbelief.

Benny was scowling. This would be the last time he called a tip line.

"Ms. Bloom, who purchased the poison and how could it end up in your baked goods?"

"Don't say a word, Star," Gran said. "Officer, I told the other officer, that I bought the bait. You can't be too careful when you're serving the public. As for any of it getting into our batter, it is absolutely impossible. Just ask your fellow officer where he found it?"

"Tell you what ... Mrs. ...

"Mary Bloom. I'm Star's grandmother."

"Okay, Mrs. Bloom, why don't you come down to the station with me, give your statement to Detective Watson. We'll bring you back." Looking at his partner poking in the cabinets, Trippy asked, "Find anything else."

"No, only that one box."

"Mrs. Bloom, come with us. We'll have to take the box, test it to see if it matches the contents in John Doe's stomach ... you know what I'm saying?"

"Yes, I know exactly what you're saying. You are accusing me of poisoning someone. It's preposterous. I'm going to report you to ... to ... my personal private investigators. Star dear, you call ... you know who I'm talking about."

"Gran, I'm sure they're not charging you with murder. Officer Trippy, can I open the shop?" Star asked.

"Not until we verify it's not the same poison we found in John Doe's stomach."

Star sighed, looking at Gran then Officer Trippy. "Please hurry. We only have one more day to fill the orders. Our customer's will be coming tomorrow afternoon to pick up their Thanksgiving trimmings."

Star slumped in the chair as a puff of air breezed in the door behind Gran and the officers. One officer carried the bagged hotels as if it was a bomb, Gran continuing her protestations.

Retrieving her phone, Star sent a quick text message to Tyler.

● ● ●

"You'll never believe what just happened. S."

Star relayed the bakery's predicament … she waited for a reply … waited.

"Ty, did you get my message? S."

"Ah, yes, sorry … I'm sketching … the little baker girl is waging a fierce battle against evil black bugs with big yellow eyes, green teeth and glowing orange horns. A swashbuckling officer, armed with a gold bat, is fighting valiantly to protect the little blonde baker girl. Sorry, I have to run. Later. T."

"Cute. Let me know if the swashbuckler wins. Have to run too. S."

• • •

STAR SNAPPED TO attention and called Liz thinking Gran's suggestion was right on point. *This is ridiculous. Taking Gran in for questioning.* She was sure their personal PIs would put an end to the harassment.

• • •

RECEIVING STAR'S CALL FOR HELP, Manny stormed into police headquarters, breezed by the window in front of an alarmed duty officer, and into Detective Watson's office. "What's with hauling a sixty-nine year old grandmother in for questioning about a box of rat poison?"

"We had to be sure the bakery wasn't involved and … it was a good lesson for your friend, Ms. Bloom, to be careful. I'll call her to explain and tell her why it was necessary … and tell her I'm sorry. But an investigation has to be thorough." Detective Watson smiled, his pearly white teeth against his black skin brought a smile from Manny.

"Yeah … well … where is Mary Bloom?"

"She's probably walking in the bakery as we speak." Pearly white teeth again.

"Well, okay. See ya." Manny showed his pearly whites back at the detective.

"See ya."

Chapter 13

A BLACK AND WHITE squad car pulled around to the back of the strip mall, rolling to a stop at the bakery. An officer hopped out, held the car door open extending a hand to his passenger. The officer said goodbye to the woman who brushed by him.

The back door to the bakery swung open and Gran strolled in, Star raced to her, folded her in her arms. "Are you all right?" Star hugged her again, kissed each cheek.

"Rather exciting, dear. But a nice hot cup of tea, chamomile I think, would help. Soothe my nerves. I hear the cash register. Are we open for business?"

"Yes. Detective Watson just called. He was sorry for any inconvenience. Can you beat that … inconvenience? I wanted to scream at him that he caused way more than an inconvenience." Star's blood pressure shocked her veins as she whirled away, took several deep breaths, slumped on a stool and looked up at Gran. "He said arsenic from rat poison was found in John Doe's stomach. Did he tell you that?"

"Yes. Poor Mr. Doe. They have no idea who he is. Benny is the only one who could shed some light and that was very little. Okay, dear, where should I start? We don't have a moment to waste. Thanksgiving pickups will start arriving before we know it."

"Wanda separated the orders into four piles—bread and cookies, pies, and cakes. We figure that whoever tackles the bread can do the cookies while the bread dough is rising. We'll all take turns decorating the cookies. If we're lucky we might finish before midnight. Then we can get a few hours of sleep before our customers start coming in tomorrow to pick up their orders."

"Okay if I take the pie orders? I love the sweet scent of mincemeat. Although I have to say, pumpkin gives me the willies today," Gran said setting up her space in the kitchen.

"What's the matter with pumpkin, Mary?" Wanda asked bumping through the doors to the kitchen with a fist full of cake orders.

"Pumpkin was found in Mr. Doe's stomach. I guess Benny gave him a spicy pumpkin cupcake." Star said.

With pumpkin cupcakes left hanging in their minds, the bakers smiled to themselves hearing *Over the River and Through the Woods to Grandmother's House We go*. Benny was feeding the Wurly again. He had spent several hours at the consignment shop down the street going through their inventory of used CDs, then loaded up the Wurlitzer with holiday music. He also requested a spray can of snow which Wanda picked up.

Benny sprayed the snow on the bottom three inches of the picture windows adding to the nostalgia of an old-fashioned bakery. The retirees from the north commented how they loved to come into the bakery with the aroma of baking bread, lace curtains, and now snow—it felt like home ... *a little.*

Star set up the mixer with a dough blade, sorted the bread orders, as her cell phone rang.

"Hello, Star's Bakery."

"Now, isn't this a treat to hear your voice, Star Bloom."

"Sorry, I don't recognize your voice. Who's calling and how can I help?"

"I'm crushed that you don't recognize my voice. Here, let me put my partner on the line."

"Hello, Miss Bloom. It's Stephanie Hall. Jim Whisk and I have wonderful news."

"Oh, my. How are you?" Star wasn't sure if she felt glad or mad to know the scoundrels were on the line, the producers who skipped town because they didn't have the prize money they owed her.

Jim was back on the line. "We're fine. Tickled pink. So glad we tracked you down. We called as soon as we received the news."

"Who is it, Star?" Gran whispered watching her granddaughter's face grow pensive. At least it wasn't more news about that poor Mr. Doe.

Star covered the receiver. "Jim Whisk and Stephanie Hall. The two producers who filmed the Amateur Bakeoff."

"You mean the show you won and the two people who skipped town without paying you the prize money? Let's see, that was fifty-thousand dollars I believe." Her voice was harsh, brows raised, head shaking. She didn't like that pair one bit.

Star nodded. "What's the news, Mr. Whisk?"

"An investor has picked up the show. He has a television syndicate that wants to run it over the holidays. So time is of the essence."

"Hold everything. Does that mean I get my prize money?"

"But, of course."

"When, Mr. Whisk?"

"Right away. I'll send you the contract via email. Now—"

"Oh, no. Money first, then I sign the new contract."

"Oh, well, that's not the way it works. Just—"

"That is the way it works, Mr. Whisk."

"Oh, well—"

Star could hear Jim and Stephanie whispering. The last time that pair huddled it was very bad news.

"Okay, Stephanie and I will arrange for you to meet the investor. He will have the money. Can you make it to Orlando this Friday?"

"No, I can't. As you have probably surmised, I was able to open my bakery, and this is a very big weekend with Thanksgiving. I could clear my schedule Monday, however." Star shared grins with Gran and Wanda.

"That's showing him," Wanda whispered.

"Okay. We think the investor will still be in Orlando. I know he's visiting family for the holiday. I'll email you the time and place. We'll shoot for Monday, late morning, say eleven o'clock. Will that be good for you?"

"Yes. I look forward to seeing you and Stephanie—with the prize money. I'll be especially happy to meet this new investor. Bye." Star couldn't help but add a sugary tone to her voice bordering on the sarcastic. She pocketed her cell. "So, Wanda, will an influx of cash, fifty thousand, help our cash flow problem?"

"What cash flow problem," Wanda replied, grinning as she began mixing the batter for a ginger-spice cake to fill the next order on her list.

Chapter 14

THE SUN WAS HIGH in the sky matching Star's soaring spirits. In spite of Detective Watson closing the shop for two hours, they had filled all the orders. Friday and Saturday following Thanksgiving, the phone had rung off the hook with holiday orders. Seems their customers were more than happy with their pies, breads, and other baked goods. They were not only placing additional orders for their holiday tables but also ordering baked goods as gifts for family and friends, as well as guests who might pop by for a glass of holiday cheer.

Wanda warned that even with the cash from Thanksgiving it was going to be almost impossible to purchase all the ingredients for the new orders. Star immediately countered that the coffers would soon receive a big bump after she met with Mr. Whisk.

Speeding west on Route 4 to Orlando, Star glanced at Gran. Their hearts were beating in unison with excitement.

"Seems like Ty's riding with us for luck, meeting only a half mile from Disney World, don't you think, Gran?"

"Yes, dear. Next exit. Exit 74A, then a left onto Turkey Lake Road. Less than a quarter mile."

"Got it," she said giggling. "Turkey Lake Road … a good luck charm along with our Thanksgiving success. You know, Gran, I really don't hold a grudge against Jim and Steph. They tried. Like they say, that's show biz—close before you even open."

"There … Dunkin' Donuts. Drive-in lane is backed up—lunchtime, I guess. There's an opening … park there, dear."

Inside the coffee shop Gran led the way to a table vacated by three young women chatting so fast they almost bumped into her as she slid into a chair. Star sat in the chair next to Gran, chuckling at her near miss. Gran picked the perfect table for an important conference—back in the corner with four chairs.

The shop was filled with animated conversations, mingling with the mouth-watering scent of fresh baked bagels and the ever famous Dunkin' coffee. Business people sharing their adventures over the long weekend. Star touched Gran's hand, nodded to the paper snowflakes stuck on the window next to their table. She thought of Benny spraying foam snow on the bakery windows.

"Want a cup of coffee, Gran. I sure want one—after an hour on the road. I have to be sharp for our meeting. We have time—twenty minutes until eleven o'clock."

"Yes. But make it a small cup or I'll get too jittery. After you get the coffees, I have to run to the restroom."

• • •

REFRESHED, SIPPING THEIR COFFEE, Star pulled out a pad of paper from her tote.

"It's nice to have a few minutes to catch our breath. We learned so much from our first two weeks. Now we have to plan for Christmas, New Years, Hanukkah, all the holidays. Maybe around December fifteenth run an ad for bakery specials. We have to create some excitement."

"I like it," Gran said, taking a sip, looking over her shoulder so she could wave down Jim and Stephanie.

"With the fifty grand we'll have some breathing room. Like Wanda said, 'what cash flow problem.' We're so lucky she joined us. I think it would be a good idea to hire some part-time help. Don't you?"

"Oh, yes. I don't think I could hold up under the pressure again—getting everything ready for the opening, then Thanksgiving … definitely need help for the upcoming holidays."

"When I was taking the baking classes, the culinary arts students were always looking for some hours to earn money. They would be a big plus—already knowing how to bake bread. Of course, they didn't have your special recipes, Gran."

"Why don't you ask Tyler about advertising?"

"Good idea. And his mom. Cindy advertises all the time for her real estate listings." Star looked at her watch.

11:15 a.m.

"I think I'll get another coffee. How about you, Gran?"

"No thanks, I can barely keep my hands from shaking as it is."

Star returned to the table with a small coffee and a plain bagel. Tearing it in half, she placed a piece on a napkin for Gran. "Eat this. It will help mop up those jitters," Star said smiling. "Do you think I have the right Dunkin'? I thought they'd be here by now."

"Check your email, dear."

"Jim didn't send an email. He left a voice-mail."

"Then his number. It should be listed on your ... shouldn't it?"

"He must have borrowed someone else's phone. I tried. They'd never heard of a Jim Whisk. You know, sometimes you have to recharge your phone so you use someone else's while you wait."

"What about his other messages when you were in the bakeoff competition?"

"I tried to send him a message a few weeks ago to see if there was any activity around the show. It came back with the dreaded *Daemon—unknown addressee*. The bakeoff website isn't available anymore."

11:30 a.m.

"Gran ... you don't suppose?"

Gran shrugged her shoulders, her eyes riveted on the door, watching customers come and customers go.

12:00 p.m.

• • •

STAR POUNDED THE STEERING wheel as the red SUV sped east on Route 4 to Daytona Beach.

"Duped again. A sucker, that's what I am, Gran. Why did I believe them? They're charlatans."

"But they wanted you to meet—"

"Meeting was my idea. The investor was to bring the money, a check, because I said I wouldn't do anything further until I had the prize money, the fifty grand, they owed me. I bet they got the money and fled, skipped town again. I just know it. I'm screwed again."

Star's phone trilled a bar of jingle bells, her new setting for the arrival of a text message.

• • •

"How did meet go? T."

"They no show. S."

"Pox on them. T."

"R U still coming home? S."

"3 weeks. Can't wait 2 see U. Chin up, Ms. Bloom. T."

Chapter 15

STAR DRAPED HER ARM around Gran's shoulders as they walked slowly up to the back door of the bakery. Neither wanted to face Wanda, neither wanted to tell her they were back empty handed. There was no fifty thousand dollars.

Sighing, hesitating, Star tried to put on a brave face as she pushed the door open stepping inside, Gran close behind. Both of their jaws dropped. The Butterworth sisters appeared to be in charge. Hattie had a smudge of flour on her nose. The frilly white apron around Mattie's waist was streaked with chocolate. Anne was calling out to Wanda asking where the rest of the spices were kept. The cinnamon jar was empty.

Wanda, answering her call for spices, hustled through the swinging doors into the kitchen to find her employers looking as if they had lost their best friend, gawking, speechless at who was in the kitchen … in aprons no less.

Wanda raced to Star giving her a tight squeeze, then squeezed Gran.

"What's going on?" Star stammered looking from sister to sister, back to Wanda.

"It's all good, Star. After you and Gran left for your meeting with the producers, I joined Benny and the Butterworth sisters for a cup of coffee. No one was in the shop. I told them how great it was that we were going to have an influx of cash, sorely needed, I told them we were swamped with orders but not enough funds to cover the ingredients. I told them I was calling the college to see if we could get some student help."

Interrupting, Anne stepped forward, always the leader for her sisters, Hattie and Mattie. "We told her to look no further. We could help in a pinch."

"We do know our way around the kitchen, Star. Maybe not creative like you," Hattie said.

"But we can crack an egg and sift some flour." Mattie added.

"That's wonderful, but you can't … we can't pay you."

"What do you mean?" Wanda asked. "With the money—"

"There isn't any money. Jim and Stephanie never showed up." Star looked at Wanda's face falling in alarm. "Gran and I think they skipped town with the money, or there never was any money, never was another investor … we don't know. But we do know we don't have a check to deposit. And … " Star sighed looked to the ceiling, fighting back tears. "And so … we can't pay you, Anne. But thank you for—"

"Poppycock. We'll consider this our next adventure. Won't we?" Anne looked at Hattie.

"Oh, yes."

"A new adventure," Mattie said a twinkle in her eyes.

"We don't make any money now … going from one adventure to another," Anne explained. "So, the way I look at it, zero plus zero equals zero. No better, but more to the point, no worse off than we were before we put on these aprons. Agree, Hattie? Mattie?"

The sisters grinned back at Anne—*so smart*. "We agree."

"Now, Wanda, where do you keep the spices?" Anne asked opening a cupboard door.

Star shook her head. "Wait, if you help us, maybe by January we'll have our heads above water enough to begin paying you. Wanda, you keep an account of the hours the Butterworth sisters work. This is a debt that we are going to pay off … pay accumulating from today."

The sisters looked wide-eyed at Wanda, waiting. Paid for an adventure? That had never happened before.

"It's a deal, provided we're still in business in January. Star, you won't believe how quickly the sisters filled the display cases—Hattie is a whiz at bread, and Mattie ... well, her cakes are beautiful. Just come with me ...

"Wanda, hold on. The rest of the spices, please! We're out of cinnamon," Anne reiterated, hands on her hips, trying hard to look stern but failing as her lips spread into a smiley face.

Ka-ching!

Star looked at Gran. Benny was out front racking up another sale.

● ● ●

JINGLE BELLS RANG OUT from Star's pocket.

"R U back at bakery? T."

"Yes. U won't believe who in kitchen. Baking! Anne, Hatt & Matt. I can't pay them. A.H.M. say don't care, S."

"Yeah! + I had call from indie film company. Interested in Baker Girl. T."

"Fingers crossed 4 U, S."

"Mine crossed 4 U, T."

Chapter 16

NIGHT HAD FALLEN, ending a day filled with bad news followed by a dramatic up tick. Star couldn't stop smiling. The crazy, wonderful Butterworth sisters jumping in to help, thrilled to be starting a new adventure. Climbing the ladder to the top bunk, Star's lips turned up in a loving smile as she gazed through the rungs at Gran. She was snoring softly exhausted from the day's bumpy ride.

Settling on her bunk images of the day raced through her mind. She was furious with Jim and Stephanie. She tried to push the no show aside but she couldn't. Climbing back down the ladder, she picked up her phone lying next to the blender, slid down on the floor hoping the counter would act as a noise buffer. She didn't want to wake Gran. Scanning her directory, she found the number and punched the entry.

"Salinas."

"Manny, I'm sorry to call so late … what was that? Sounded like a baby. Where are you?"

"I'm at the hospital. I'm pushing speaker. I want you to congratulate my beautiful, incredible, fantastic wife on giving me a baby girl."

Star could hear Manny struggling to keep his composure.

"She's perfect. The cutest little six-pound baby girl with a mop of red curls."

"Liz, Liz, can you hear me?" Star squealed into the phone forgetting about Gran.

"Yes, Star. We hear you. My dear husband is exaggerating, but I like to hear his words just the same."

"I thought you had a couple more weeks before the baby was due?"

"Me too. But little Lizzie decided it was time to meet her mommy and daddy. What's up with you?"

"Oh, not now. You two must be exhausted. We can talk tomorrow?"

"Nonsense," Manny said. "I can look at Liz and Lizzie while you talk. Give it to us. Can't vouch for what we might say. Might be a little incoherent."

Star filled Manny and Liz in on what had transpired, mainly the no show meaning no money ... again. "I don't suppose there's any way to make them cough it up. Of course, it may have all been a ruse, even a misunderstanding on my part that I was actually going to meet the investor and that they really said they would have the money."

Star looked up as Gran slid down next to her on the floor, leaned against the cabinet. "Liz had her baby. Liz and Manny are both on the phone," she whispered. "In the hospital."

"Do you have an email address? Anything from the bakeoff?" Manny asked. "Telephone number they called you from?"

"No, no, and no. Liz, Gran is here by my side."

"Liz, dear, congratulations. When was the baby born?"

"Early this morning. She'll be a whole day old in a few hours. Imagine that."

"That's wonderful, dear. Are you all right? How are you feeling?"

"I'm wonderful. Everything is fine—I counted her fingers and toes several—"

"I counted them, too," Manny chimed in. "Star, I doubt there is anything you can do about those two scoundrels. Text me their names and I'll see if I can find them, if any luck, at least I can ask them a few questions. Scare them a little. But probably not enough to cough up the money."

"Thanks, and there's no hurry. As the Butterworth sisters said today—zero plus zero is still zero."

"Butterworth sisters?" Liz asked.

"I'll fill you in later. We love you both, make that we love the three of you."

Liz spoke up. "You'll be little Lizzie's first case."

"Yeah, learning at her papa's knee."

"I beg your pardon, my dear husband."

"Make that her mama's and her papa's knees."

Chapter 17

THE NEXT DAY no one mentioned the words *prize money* in front of Star. Privately, however, they whispered that if the reality-TV pair ever dared to enter the bakery they would tie them up and call the police, or something worse.

Wanda made up a work schedule for the burgeoning staff. Drawing lines, setting hourly timeslots then penciled in Benny, the sisters, as well as herself, Gran, and Star. Not happy with the result, basically tearing her hair out, she tried again to come up with a plan only to wad up the sheet and start again … and again.

In order to get the fresh baked goods from oven, to slotted trolley, to the display cases in the front of the store, they had to start baking at 5:00 a.m. The bakery would close at 6:00 p.m. Star told Wanda the bakery would be closed on Monday and Tuesday. They would also close on all major holidays. With *days closed* established everyone could make their personal plans for the week, the holidays.

Wanda sighed. Triumphant. She finally came up with a schedule so that only two sisters would come in at 5:00 with Star. Gran and Wanda and a sister would show up at 8:45 a.m. to open at 9:00. However, before declaring the schedule was final, she was going to keep a tally, make that ask Benny to keep a tally of customer traffic. Did traffic really begin to build at ten o'clock not nine? If so, she would skew the whole schedule up an hour.

If the weather was prohibitive in the morning, which she positively swore rarely happened on Florida's central east coast, Benny would catch a ride with whatever sister came in at 8:45.

At any rate, that was the timetable. Gran liked the schedule but she knew that her granddaughter would put in twelve hour days, make that thirteen, but with the car she could scoot home on slow days to rest. Star and Gran stayed out of the schedule negotiations knowing they would take care of each other's comings and goings. The whole schedule thing ended with giggling fits when they laid their heads on their pillows—upper and lower bunk.

The first day they tried the new schedule everyone, except Mattie and Benny, showed up at 5:00. Mattie left the house at 8:00, drove the sister's SUV to pick up Benny. But Benny was already motoring down Atlantic Avenue in his wheelchair, a new ball cap pulled low over his bushy salt and pepper hair missing a lock or two, thinking he wouldn't be recognized. But he didn't fool Mattie for a minute. She pulled a U-turn, rolled up to the curb beside Benny.

Irritated that she had seen through his disguise, Benny waved her on as he whizzed by.

Stepping on the gas, Mattie passed him, leaving him to travel on his own up the sidewalk.

Benny's routine, sitting in the window of the bakery with his coffee and newspaper, meant he had to be at the bakery no later than 8:30 because the schedule showed he was to be at the cash register at nine sharp. He certainly didn't need help after being on his own since leaving his foster home at seventeen to join the circus. He muttered that a fifty-nine year old man did not need three mothers. It was humiliating. His lips turned down under the tufts of gray hair on his chin. *Humiliating!*

The second day ran smoother except that Anne didn't want to leave her sisters alone for the morning baking. When Hattie and Mattie threatened Anne with mutiny, the day went according to schedule, with one of the sisters swapping with the other. After all, Wanda said anytime they wanted, they should make their own schedule as long as the bakery was staffed according to the timetable. Anne, huddling with her sisters, gave an edict that the three would bake together. Relieved, the three went back to sifting, stirring, cracking eggs.

Benny stated he was fine under his own steam, so to speak, unless he called for a pick up.

With order returning, Anne bustled out to the car retrieving six bags, a name pinned on the front of each. Striding back she joined her two sisters, all three looking like feral cats that caught a gecko. Anne handed the bags out according to the name on the front. Benny opened his first. A toothy grin spreading across his face, he pulled out a white T-shirt, *Star's Bakery* imprinted in black across the front. Dropping the red suspenders from his shoulders, he pulled the shirt over the yellow one he was wearing.

Star opened her bag next, withdrawing a black T-shirt with *Star's Bakery* imprinted in white. The sisters and Wanda opened their bags—black short-sleeved T-shirts with white lettering. Anne explained that Benny was special, so his was white. Besides, black would show up better when the women tied on their frilly white aprons out in the shop helping customers.

• • •

TYLER SMILED, his pencil moving furiously over the pad of paper after reading Star's text describing the chaos that ensued with Wanda's work schedule. Cartoons danced across the page— Benny, his salt and pepper hair bouncing from under his cap as he raced the Butterworth sister down the street; the little blonde baker girl grinning out at him wearing her new shirt; then another with the sisters, Gran, and Wanda nudging each other, giggling, as the Wurlitzer sprouted stick arms and legs performing a wild tango with each baker—dips, and twirls.

Chapter 18

THE MERRY BAND of bakers settled into Wanda's routine— *everyone doing their own thing.* Of course, all choosing to be at the bakery at the same time for fear they'd miss a drop of gossip.

Holding the phone under her chin, Star answered as she continued to frost cutouts of a Christmas Tree. "Star's Bakery. How may I help you?"

"Star Bloom, please."

"This is Star. Who's calling?"

"Where have you been, young lady? I've been trying to find you."

"I'm sorry. Do I know you?"

"My name is Vincent Roth. I'm a producer for CBS affiliates— always on the lookout for something new. I thought I found a new production but then Mr. Jim Whisk vanished, or isn't interested, or … anyway—"

"Mr. Roth, I doubt we have anything to say to each other. I met with Mr. Whisk, or rather, I was supposed to meet with Mr. Whisk when he promised he would give me the fifty thousand dollars prize money he owes me for winning the Amateur Bakeoff Competition last August."

"I don't understand. I wired Mr. Whisk the money. Are you telling me he didn't give it to you?"

"Yes, Mr. Roth. That is exactly what I'm telling you. Now if you'll excuse me, I have some Christmas trees in the oven, and—"

"Wait, Miss. Bloom. It seems we both have been swindled, but I should have known better. I'm going to call my bank, and the police, and ... and a detective to find Mr. Whisk. Oh, how stupid can I be? When I talked with Mr. Whisk, I told him I was interested in the show, and that I wanted to meet with you ... he said you would not meet unless you were paid the prize money. He said he didn't have the money because of production costs for the series, and that investors did not come through. I'm sorry, I was very excited with the potential of ... thank heavens I insisted he send me the files of the Amateur Bakeoff ... so, I guess I did get something for my fifty grand."

"Mr. Roth, I don't know why you're calling, but I can tell you positively that I want nothing more to do with Mr. Whisk, or the reality show."

"Look, Miss Bloom, I understand your misgivings, but I assure you that I'm sincere when I say I am interested in syndicating the series. And, depending on how the series is received, I'm also very interested in you. Can you come to Los Angeles so we can talk face to face? I want to give you my thoughts on how we might work together, go forward together. I definitely want you to take a screen test."

"A screen test? Mr. Roth, I don't doubt your sincerity, but I can't pay for a trip to LA with *your sincerity*. I think—"

"Miss Bloom, I will make a reservation, round trip, pay for the flight and hotel as well as give you an expense account which I will cover from the moment you leave your home until you step back into your home. Please, Miss Bloom. From what I've seen, the camera loves you. We must talk in person and, unfortunately, I can't get away until the first of the year. I don't want to wait that long. What do you say?"

The camera loves you. My God, those were Ty's words. I could see Ty ... all expenses paid. "You are very persuasive, Mr. Roth. One question. Should you decide the camera doesn't love me, will you still pay for my trip? Door to door?"

"Yes, yes, Miss Bloom. Door to door."

"It's a long distance to Los Angeles, Mr. Roth. I can only manage to be away from my bakery for two days—I'll have to take the red eye."

"Whatever you say, Miss Bloom. If you want to fly all night, then that's what you'll do. Please pick your airline, email me the dates, flight numbers, and I'll make your reservations. You just have to arrive at the airport. Your ticket will be prepaid. I'm emailing you as we speak, so you have my address. Also, the email will have my direct line. Do you have a PayPal account?"

"Yes, I do."

"Good. I'll send the advance to your account to cover your initial expenses as soon as your flight plans are settled, plus information on how to submit your expense account. Thank you, Miss Bloom. When do you think I can expect you?"

"In two days. The holidays are coming up and I have to tend to my business. The final date and times will be in my return email to you."

• • •

TAPPING HER TOES, waiting, waiting for Ty to pick up his phone, Star glanced at the clock, glanced again ... *where is he?*

"Star, Star hold on, I'm here. Heard your ring tone from down the hall."

"Oh ... I was afraid you were ... never mind. Guess what just happened?"

"I can't. Tell me," Tyler said gasping for breath.

"A Mr. Roth, a producer, just called. He wants to meet with me, wants me to take a screen test, he's sending money to PayPal for heaven sake and—"

"Slower. Meet where?"

"L A!" Star practically screamed, jumping up from her chair.

"Los Angeles?" Tyler gasped.

"Yes." Star gasped back at him.

"Wow! When?"

"I ... I think I'll fly day after tomorrow."

"O my God. I'll meet your flight. How long can you stay? Please say a week."

"No, silly. Two days."

Chapter 19

Dallas, Texas

LOUISE WAINWRIGHT SIPPED her morning coffee, glancing between the morning newspaper on her iPad and the sun breaching the horizon, the rays spreading over Dallas lying out below her penthouse. A new email pinged her inbox. It was from Lou, her daughter, married ten months to Thom Weed. Lou still considered herself a newlywed, still breathless over her *dreamy* husband. Louise wondered how long the marriage was going to last. Although she was fond of her new son-in-law, the thought remained—did Thom marry her daughter for her potential inheritance? Louise often wondered the same about Jude, her husband.

Ah, yes, Jude. She heard him shuffling down the hall for his morning cup of coffee. *Will he find a job today?* At the urging of her father, when she married Jude Rattigan, she didn't take his name, opting to keep her maiden name—Wainwright. Louise didn't see the warning signs her father spotted before she married Jude. After their daughter was born and his lack of interest in the baby, Louise saw what her father saw. But Jude was attentive, and handsome with thick, wiry black hair. He was an attentive escort to the various charity functions in which she was deeply involved. Oh, she knew he had dalliances, but preferred to look the other way as long as he kept them undercover, so to speak.

Sighing, Louise turned back to the newspaper, flicking the pages with her finger on the touch screen, always looking for a chance article about her father. She and her father had been estranged because of his weird lifestyle, some called strange, and his lengthy disappearances. However, he was in the habit of sending postcards at random intervals, from random places, never giving a return address. For all she knew, he could be somewhere in the city, sending a card to a faraway colleague, anywhere in the world, and asking the colleague to post the card. A postcard could land in her mailbox two weeks in a row, or months apart. Louise was a psychiatrist and she long ago had labeled her father very eccentric but with a mind sharp as a tack. Because it had been eight months since she had heard from him she had hired an investigator to begin a missing-person search.

Later, when she thought back to this moment, she didn't know why her eye caught a word on the screen. She had already flicked past the page but returned. The word was buried in two short paragraphs—*Yamamoto*. She smiled thinking of her father. Yohji Yamamoto was her father's favorite designer, used to be anyway. Louise remembered a delightful dinner, actually two dinners—one in Paris, the other in Tokyo.

Louise scanned the article. The police were looking for someone who could identify a John Doe. They guessed his age to be sixty-five to seventy-five, with light gray hair, wearing a jacket by designer Yohji Yamamoto. His body was found on the waterfront in Daytona Beach. It was believed he might be from Texas.

Louise gasped, her hand clutching her chest. *His body was found … his dead body was found?* The thought had occurred to her that her father's long absence could mean he was sick. This time his absence could mean he met with foul play. Should she get in touch with her investigator?

She read the article again. There was a number to call if anyone had information that might lead to John Doe's identity ... no matter how insignificant—call! Daytona Beach?

Florida! When she was ten, her mother and father had taken her to Orlando, to Disney World. It was one of her fondest memories of her mother. She died four years later of cancer. As a doctor of psychiatry, looking back, Louise wondered if her mother's death, which might have brought father and daughter closer, had served instead to push them apart.

Well, it couldn't hurt to call. With a complete description of this John Doe, it would no doubt eliminate her father.

Louise made a note of the telephone number.

Jude massaged her neck as he gazed over her shoulder at her computer screen. "You're going to call? Why?"

"It's been so long since I've seen Dad. I've been wondering if something happened. I'm sure this John Doe isn't him, but I might as well call. Eliminate the possibility."

"That's silly, Louise. The old codger is probably on some Hawaiian beach with a woman."

"Why would you say that, Jude?"

Jude walked to the window, looked down at the city. "No reason. You say he's eccentric, call his lifestyle strange."

Louise glanced at her watch. She was going to be late for her first appointment if she didn't hurry.

• • •

LOUISE FINISHED WRITING her observations on the session with her last patient. Pulling the note she had jotted down that morning from the police article, she tapped in the numbers.

"Daytona Beach Police Department. Can I help you?"

"I'm calling about an article I saw in the Dallas Morning News, about a John Doe."

"Your name please?"

"Dr. Louise Wainwright, but I—"

"One moment, I'll connect you to Detective Watson."

"But—"

"Detective Watson here. Dr. Wainwright do you believe you have some information on my John Doe?"

"Detective, I doubt it. It's just that the man's jacket, the Yohji Yamamoto jacket. He was my father's favorite designer."

"You live in Dallas?"

"Yes."

"Is your father missing?"

"Well, not exactly. That is ... we are rather estranged. He sends me postcards from time to time, but I haven't heard from him for about eight months."

"Dr. Wainwright is this a good number to call you on?"

"Yes, it's my cell phone, but—"

"I'd like a private investigator, assigned to this case, to give you a call. His name is Manny Salinas. You're probably right ... not your father ... but we haven't been able to turn up any clues as to John Doe's identity." Fred chuckled. "At least I can report to my captain that someone inquired."

Chapter 20

Los Angeles, California

HER HEART TICKED UP a beat as she jockeyed in line with the other passengers waiting for the plane's door to open, allowing them to escape the stifling air. Finally, there was movement.

Star walked out of the jetway with the rest of the crowd, her heart thumping. In a few minutes she would see Tyler. They had exchanged several text messages since her call.

He said he'd meet her with open arms.

Nerves gripped her senses remembering his passionate kiss only two weeks ago when they said goodbye at the Orlando airport. He was returning to California after his surprise visit as Superman at the grand opening of her bakery. She could feel her face flushing just thinking about how she responded, how her whole body responded to his embrace. She knew he was coming home for Christmas, but now here she was, unexpectedly in California.

Wanda had dropped her off at the airport. With the sun following her, she was now in Los Angeles a little after 9:00 a.m. Her appointment with Mr. Roth was at noon. She asked to meet early as she would be her freshest at the beginning of her journey. But, the real reason was because that would give her the rest of the day with Tyler, and most of the following day. She was scheduled on the red-eye back to Florida the following night.

Flying non-stop, flying from night to day, was the only way she could justify being away from the bakery with the orders piling up for the holidays. Tyler had suggested she eat something on the plane even if she wasn't hungry so she would have strength for the meeting with Roth and the pressure of a screen test. He was driving her to the meeting at Roth's studio and would wait for her at a coffee shop nearby. Tyler didn't want to take any chances on making her nervous. Roth had booked her a room in a hotel, at her request, not far from Tyler's one-bedroom apartment.

Tyler was taking the two days off, the only days he hadn't worked since leaving Florida two months ago. They would relax, see the sights, and talk, talk, talk.

These thoughts swarmed through her head as her eyes sought Tyler out through the crowd.

He spotted her first, waved, called to her, opening his arms as she rushed forward. Lifting her in the air she dropped the handle of her carry-on, laughing. Setting her on her feet, he grasped the handle of her suitcase, pulling it and her close. Their embrace didn't last long with the other passengers bumping around them to retrieve their bags circling on the track of the luggage carousel.

Releasing her, a final peck on her luscious lips, an arm around her shoulders, he nodded to the passing luggage. "Did you check a suitcase?"

"Nope. This is it."

"Okay, let's get of here." Leading her to the parking garage exit, he stopped for a quick kiss … smiling, continued walking. "How was your flight?"

"Not bad, but this is better."

● ● ●

WHIZZING OUT OF THE AIRPORT, Tyler deftly navigated the highway, the streets, and before she could think Tyler had escorted her to Roth's building, his lobby. Identifying herself to the receptionist, and her appointment with Mr. Roth, she looked over her shoulder at Ty. He flashed her a *thumbs up*.

The receptionist escorted Star to a small conference room. The side table was set with a carafe of coffee and several blueberry muffins. Roth followed her into the room, pumping her hand in greeting.

"Miss Bloom, thank you for coming so quickly. How was your flight?"

Star was relieved to see that Roth was an older gentleman, about the age of her father—fifty-five. His dark brown hair was streaked with gray, held back in a short ponytail. His manner was friendly, and he seemed genuinely glad to see her. All pluses. As far as Star was concerned it didn't matter what happened with Roth because his call resulted in a free trip to California to see Tyler.

"Smooth, thank you, sir."

Roth chuckled. "Cup of coffee? And please, call me Vincent. May I call you Star?"

"Of course … Vincent. And, I'll pass on the coffee." She was afraid that another jolt of caffeine would give her the jitters, and she didn't want to excuse herself to run to the restroom.

Roth helped himself to coffee and then the two of them sat across from each other at the golden oak conference table.

"You mentioned on the phone that you were trying to find Jim Whisk and his co-producer. Any chance I'll be given the prize money, the fifty thousand?" Star asked.

"Nothing yet. I learned he picked up the wire-transfer within minutes of our bank sending it. I'm sorry, Star, I wish I could come up with another fifty grand, but I can't. I will let you know the minute we track him, or her down." Roth paused, took a sip of coffee, a smile spreading across his face. "Let's talk about you today. I just finished viewing, again, the bakeoff episode where you were sitting on the floor watching your oven. It was hilarious, but I'm sure you didn't see it that way at the time. It was the pie episode I believe. I'll never look at a pie with a crust without wondering if I'll find a soggy bottom."

Star laughed with him. "You're right. It was not funny at the time."

"Why don't we film your screen test, get that out of the way, and then we can chat. Is that okay with you?"

"Yes, I'd prefer that, although my dress might be a little wrinkled. I didn't have time to freshen up, or change."

"Not a problem. I thought about a five-minute clip on making taffy. Since taffy gave you your big win in the competition, I was sure you could describe—"

"Taffy will be a perfect subject. Do you have a kitchen?"

Roth chuckled again. "No, not a kitchen—a table in the center of a room with cabinets against the wall behind. I'll sit in the back so you can pretend you're making the taffy for me, make believe you have whatever you are talking about on the table in front of you."

Star thought about the sacks of sugar and flour that Ty set up on a chair as stand-ins for Benny and the Butterworth sisters.

"The purpose is to see how you come across on the screen, how you project … your voice. Is that okay?"

"Oh, yes, that's fine," she said smiling.

Roth escorted her into a small studio, introduced her to a cameraman, and then set the stage—where she should stand, where he would be. It was a little like Tyler's kitchen at home when he filmed her for the video, required to enter the bakeoff competition, except now the equipment was imaginary. No problem. She'd been making taffy in her dreams for years. She also decided to think of Roth as Benny to complete her personal stage.

Five minutes turned into ten. Roth called, "cut" to the cameraman ending the session. He motioned for her to come around to the other side of the camera, stand with him for a few minutes to see the results of the test. What did she think of it? Was she satisfied?

She nodded. Nothing seemed amiss and she doubted she could drum up the adrenalin to shoot it again. Roth seemed to agree, escorting her back to the conference room. This time she accepted his offer of coffee.

"Star, the reality show will fit nicely into one of the affiliate's holiday programming schedule, and if it doesn't air then it will run in January or February. I can't promise anything after the airing of the bakeoff competition. Some depends on how the ratings build from the first episode to the finale. But some of the other shows my company is planning to pitch would include contracting you to a spring lineup, a series of baking shows. That would mean filming in February, so we have time to cut the show to fit in a time slot. This could spawn guest appearances with some local television networks, and hopefully an interview or two as a guest on a major news show like Good Morning America. If the Bakeoff series is a success, many spots featuring you will pop up."

"Mr. Roth, where would all of this take place, provided the Bakeoff is some kind of a hit?"

"Here, in Los Angeles. The guest interviews could be anywhere—here or even New York City. If we do a pilot of your own show ... that would be here, of course."

"I don't know how all this works, but would you be asking me to move here? My bakery—"

"Not necessarily, but it is a long commute from Florida." Roth chuckled. "We would try to group the filming—could be in two-week chunks. But we're getting ahead of ourselves. One thing I can tell you is that if we are going to make you an offer, it will be by the first week in the new year."

Chapter 21

TYLER PACED THE LOBBY waiting for Star. His heart, his nerves whipping up bats in his stomach—everything inside his body jogging, bumping around. Seeing her walk off the plane, holding her in his arms, no matter how brief, was unbelievably wonderful and terrifying at once. He thought he saw it in her eyes, felt the slight quiver in her body when he hugged her.

Now what?

He was sure she would be at least an hour with Mr. Roth, what with a screen test and all. He'd learned a lot in the three months he'd been in California rubbing elbows with wannabe actors and actresses and the myriad of wannabe graphic artists and cartoon illustrators. He wondered what Star would think of the glitz, the pace, but more important how did she feel about him? Did he have a chance with her?

God, she was beautiful, cute, soft, warm—all in one package. He would do anything for her as he had the moment she first entered the diner eight months ago. Seeing her walk up to him at the airport he knew he loved her more than life itself. He had to be careful not to come on too strong, not to spook her if she wasn't ready to spend time, to spend a lifetime with him.

Glancing at his watch, he decided he had a few minutes to get some air, better to pace on the sidewalk. The receptionist was watching him. He didn't like that. His face, his body displaying a lovesick man reduced to jelly when he kissed Star on the cheek, before she turned, followed a woman sent out to escort her to meet with Mr. Roth.

• • •

TYLER STARED OUT the lobby's plate-glass window, arms crossed over his chest, commanding his feet not to take another step. He saw his reflection—khaki trousers, white golf shirt. He swiped at the lock of brown hair perpetually falling over his forehead.

He knew she was there before he heard her soft voice saying thank you to her escort.

Turning, she was stepping quickly to him. The screen test must have gone well, there was a big smile under her sparkling sky-blue eyes, or maybe her sparkling eyes were for him.

They both glanced at the receptionist, smiled, nodded, and walked out into the warm LA sun laughing over their private joke of leaving Miss Reception in the dust.

Taking her hand, Tyler guided her up the sidewalk.

"Where are we going? I have so much to tell you," she said, swinging in front of him, stepping back to his side.

"You must be hungry—"

"Starved. I had to force a muffin down on the plane."

Raising her hand to his lips, he planted a quick kiss on her knuckles. "How's this for a plan? It's less than fifteen minutes to Burbank. Drive by where I work … I don't want to go in … not sharing a minute of you with anyone else. Stop at my apartment. Then I thought we'd drive to Santa Monica—the ocean. Then back to your hotel in LA, or—"

"Isn't your car parked in the other direction?"

"Oh, yeah … or you can check in to your hotel now—"

"I like your plan A with one exception."

"That is?"

"Can we stop for lunch in Burbank then go to the ocean?"

Tyler glanced down, his eyes travelling over her face—blue eyes to pouty lips. He traced her pink lipstick with his finger, then his lips softly touched hers. Looking up with a nervous, self-conscious chuckle, "Lunch it is, Miss Bloom."

Driving up to his apartment building he glanced at Star out of the corner of his eye. He couldn't get enough of her. She was pretty before, but today, a white halter dress, she was more beautiful than any picture of Marilyn Monroe. She explained to Ty on the drive to Burbank that she chose white hoping to look like a baker for the screen test. She didn't know if Roth would ask her to wear something else, so she decided white was safe.

Tyler swallowed. She looked nothing like a baker.

Walking up the flight of stairs to his apartment neither spoke, images spinning in their minds of the hours they spent together in his studio over his parent's garage working on her video for the competition. He opened the door nodding for her to enter. A quick glance and she laughed. "Not quite like mom and dad's is it. A futon?" She glanced back at Ty. "As you know I have a futon but I don't think I told you, with money so tight, prohibiting Gran and I to move to an apartment with walls, as she likes to say, Gran bought a set of bunk beds from the consignment shop down the street. I sleep on the top bunk. I see you have your computer set up same as at home."

"The bathroom is behind that door if you want to freshen up. Clean towels are on the bar."

"Thanks. I'll just be a minute and then can we get some lunch?" she called out turning the water on in the sink.

"How about a milkshake from the deli next door to stave off the hunger pangs? Then we'll go on to Santa Monica, less than thirty minutes. I have a place in mind for lunch that I think you'll enjoy, on the water, like the Crab Shack in Daytona Beach … but different. There's even a Ferris wheel … and a rollercoaster."

"There, I feel tons better with a clean face," Star said stepping out of the bathroom. "I'm ready for whatever is pinging around in that head of yours, Mr. Jackman. No make that Superman," she said softly rising up on tiptoe to receive his kiss.

Chapter 22

Santa Monica, California

STAR COULDN'T HAVE ASKED for a more perfect day—bright sun sparking off ocean waves, new sights, but best of all she was with Tyler. Walking down the Santa Monica pier, she grabbed Ty's hand for fear she'd bump into someone as she gaped at all the attractions, the shops and specialty restaurants. Leading her back to the entrance of the pier, he opened the door to The Lobster. Out of the several dining rooms, he chose the bar with windows spanning two walls—a spectacular view of the Pacific Ocean from one, and from the other the amusement rides including a roller coaster and Ferris wheel.

"Now, Miss Bloom, relax and enjoy the view of the ocean on the west coast. Eat hearty because we'll have a late dinner."

"My stomach is a bit jumpy, maybe a salad … order for me, please."

"How about blackened salmon over a Greek Salad? It's going on four o'clock … are you faint? I'm sorry, the milkshake wasn't enough. We should have stopped in LA after your screen test—"

"No, no. It hit the spot." Her fingers sought his hand across the table, grounding her, same as when they walked down the pier fearing she'd lose him.

Smiling, Ty squeezed her hand, giving their order to the waitress.

Both were caught in the moment—they were together, the miles between no longer an obstacle. It was nice to share small talk—Star pointing out the window, chattering, asking questions about what came into view, Tyler answering, drinking in her presence.

Hungrier than they thought, it wasn't long before their salads were finished.

Drinking the last drop of her ice tea, Star glanced again at the beach, the surf. "This is breathtaking. Do you come here often?"

"Only once. It was a Sunday. A group of us had been working long hours—stopping around one in the morning, back by sunrise. The big boss ordered us to take some hours off. There are a couple of other graphic cartoonists who joined the company at the same time as I did … on this big project. So, one of the natives said we had to visit Santa Monica. I thought you'd like it. Kinda like Daytona Beach, but bigger."

"I'll say bigger. That rollercoaster is a monster."

"We'll take a ride if you like. I thought the beach, after the sun goes down, after dinner, look at the stars."

"It's wonderful … everything you said."

Tyler reached across the table for her hand. He had to touch her. "Let's walk shall we? I can't sit still—there's so much I want to show you, ask you …

"Can we go down by the rides? You said there was a carousel, then maybe the beach?"

"Sure, come on. The carousel it is. It's in the Hippodrome."

Mixing with a small crowd of children tugging the hands of their parents to hurry, Star looked up at the large tan building— eves, rounded palladium windows and doors outlined with dark blue paint. They were next in line as the carousel's horses, two sleighs, along with a goat and rabbit, slowed to a stop. Calliope organ music played, *Somewhere My Love,* as families, kids of all ages, climbed aboard.

Ty helped Star up on a big white horse, his wood saddle carved over a blanket painted blue, the bridle in gold leaf. Tyler stood, his hands on the horse's gleaming white neck, stood looking up at Star as the carousel came to life. Round and round they went, organ music filling the vast interior of the Hippodrome.

The carousel slowed, Tyler gave her a hand down, held her in his arms, a soft kiss on the lips she offered to him.

• • •

THEY RODE THE FERRIS WHEEL, screamed on the roller coaster careening down the track, clung to the crash bar rounding the bends.

They laughed at the clowns, snapped selfies with Tyler's phone, another with her phone. They browsed, stopped in the shops.

He chose an intimate restaurant for dinner, but still one with a view of the ocean. Over a chilled glass of white wine and coconut batter shrimp, the pair talked, sharing their feelings, exchanging pent-up thoughts since they parted last.

Finishing their shrimp, a second glass of wine, Ty laid his hand over hers.

He sighed, "Okay, Miss Bloom. The sun is setting. Perfect evening for the beach. I saw a shop with towels for sale. Let's pick up a couple, go down to the beach and lie on the sand, watch the stars pop out in the sky. See if they are as bright as the ones we saw that night lying on the sand in Daytona Beach."

Within fifteen minutes they were lying side by side on colorful Santa Monica emblazoned beach towels, looking up at the blanket of stars in the night sky. They didn't speak, luxuriating on the warmth of the sand, the sound of the surf.

Tyler fished for her hand. "How is everything going … back home?"

"Ty, you go first. Do you like the project, the people? I bet you're the best."

"It's fun, stimulating. I'm learning so much. At first I felt I was way over my head, but then I realized we were all on about the same level. What's interesting is how one says something, an idea on how to make the characters more lifelike. Then another one of us adds to what the first said and so on. But you know what I like the best?" Tyler leaned up on his elbow, his fingers tracing down her arm.

"What?" Shivers shot up her arm at his touch.

"The Little Baker Girl. I've added to it and … guess what?" He laid his head back on the towel.

"What?" she asked giggling.

"There's more interest. Another producer is looking at it. Maybe releasing it on New Year's Day, or some Sunday, as a short film leading to the main show. You know, parents looking for something special in the theaters instead of football on television. Especially nice for kids … all ages."

"Ty, that's wonderful."

Ty swallowed. "Star, how about we stay here tonight, in Santa Monica? I spotted a bed and breakfast when we drove in … not take you back to LA?"

Star's breathing stopped. Was he saying what she thought he was saying … not the words … the meaning? Spend the night with each other? Oh, how she wanted to. She wanted to be in his arms. She couldn't speak, could only nod, yes.

• • •

TYLER CLOSED THE DOOR to their room, turned to Star. Her shoulder bag slid to the floor as he slowly enveloped her in his arms, strong arms, his lips bending down to her lips.

Star felt the heat rising from her toes, her legs, her stomach, heart, face. Her legs were buckling, she knew she couldn't trust them another second.

Ty lifted her, laid her on the bed. How did he do that so easily, so gently? Because he was Superman, of course. He was her Superman.

Ty lay next to her drawing her close, their kisses soft, warm … turned hot, urgent. Her mind numbed, aware that her halter dress was slithering down from her neck. She was aware of his whispering as he kissed her neck. His whispers that she was *so beautiful*, that he loved her.

Love? Oh yes, she loved him, had wanted to be his for so long … saying goodbye when she took him to the airport … saying goodbye as he turned to leave. She wanted to cry out to him … *don't go*. And now, here he was, beside her.

What? What?

His shirt, trousers dropped to the floor, shoes, then socks.

Now he was lying beside her again, their bodies touching, hearts beating with desire.

The ocean was pounding outside the open French doors or was that her heart as hot sensations spread through her body. At the same passion filled moment, both breathy, said *protection*! Ty fumbled in the bed for the condom packet, ripped it open.

He turned back to Star. He kissed her, gazed into her eyes, kissed again. Oh, she prayed she was not a disappointment to him. She wanted to be everything for him. She wanted to fill his every need, desire. Because … she loved him … loved him so much. The heat rose until she couldn't bear it … rose higher … higher still.

"I love you, Star." He cried out the words for the world to hear.

"I love you," she cried out to him, again, and again.

They clung to each other, not wanting to let go, ever, ever.

Chapter 23

TWENTY-FOUR HOURS since she landed in Los Angeles, stepped into Tyler's open arms, and performed a screen test for Mr. Roth.

Twenty-four hours ago she wondered what it would be like to lay in Ty's arms, what it would be like if he made love to her.

Now she knew.

Her world had tilted. Everything that was twenty-four hours ago was now different. The sun was brighter, the raspberry jam on her muffin sweeter.

Ty loved her.

She loved him.

Tyler hustled down the hall to the inn's dining room, fixed a tray of coffee, a bowl of cut melons with strawberries and blueberries, and two muffins. Returning to their room he joined Star on the private patio, setting the tray on a small table. He squatted beside her chair, picked up her hand. "I love you, Star."

She bent down, grazed her lips over his. "I love you too."

He smiled, sitting across the little table from her, fixing her a plate. "Okay, now it's your turn. The screen test sounds promising. The producer thought he'd be back to you after the holidays. So, how about the bakery? I have to show you the cartoon I drew after I read your text that the Butterworth sisters and Benny were volunteering to help. I'm thinking of adding it to The Little Baker Girl—black shirts with Star's Bakery printed on their chests."

"The bakery is chugging along. But ...

"But?"

Star gazed out at the ocean. "Money is tight. We're barely making it. Thanksgiving orders were through the roof. We're using the influx of cash to gear up for the holidays ... after that, I don't know. Gran is worn out. She's dropping hints that maybe it's time she should return to Hoboken. But when I ask her if she wants to leave, she insists on staying. That I misunderstood her."

"If the issues with the bakery were resolved, what would you like to do? What do you dream of doing? Once, it was the bakery—"

"Yes, but what if Roth wants to hire me for a show?"

"Is that your dream? What if the job was in Daytona Beach?"

"I guess it would be exciting ... I could do both ...maybe."

"Beyond the show—say, you're a big success, then what?"

She didn't answer. She didn't know.

After satisfying their hunger with the bowl of fruit and muffins at the inn, they walked down the Third Street promenade. The atmosphere was festive—tourists gathering in the warmth of the late morning sunshine. Musicians and mimes were already out. A variety of shops were open, people browsing, buying trinkets and souvenirs.

The lovers strolled along, Ty's arm draped around her shoulders, or waist, or hands clasped swinging between them.

Star stopped at a little bakery. The door was propped open. "Can we go in here a minute?"

Ty nodded, he would wait for her at the open-air café next door.

The manager of the bakery hurried up to Star. "Can I help you with something?"

"Your bread smells wonderful. Sour dough?"

"Yes, our specialty. Can I wrap up a loaf for you?"

"Not just now. I was walking by. Is this your bakery?"

"Oh, no. The owner is running an errand. Seems there is always something he needs, or that he runs out of. I don't know how he keeps going."

"Thank you for your time. I love your shop."

Star stepped out the door, paused, seeing Ty drawing on the back of the café's paper placemat, a remnant of fudge on a napkin. He was intent on his sketch, a shock of his dark brown hair falling forward to his brow.

Sliding onto the chair beside him, exchanging a quick delicious kiss of chocolate fudge, she looked at his latest cartoon. It was a little girl sitting on a big white horse, the carousel horse. She was smiling, her eyes shining as she looked across at a little boy riding a horse next to her.

Tipping her head, Star studied his drawing. "Ty, I want to publish a children's cookbook. An e-book. A talking e-book. A little girl talking out of the screen to another child, girl or boy, showing how to scramble an egg, mix batter for a cupcake, bake it, frost it, lick the chocolate off the wooden spoon. Your cartoons … could you bring the little girl to life? To talk?"

"Sure, little Star—"

"Oh, perfect. Manny and Liz just had a baby girl. She has red ringlets. We'll call your little cartoon person Lizzie and her red—"

"Oh, no. My little baker girl is a blonde and her name is Star."

"No problem," Star said smugly. "Your little baker girl is Star, and my little baker girl, a teacher, is Lizzie with red ringlets."

"Okay. That works."

"See there, our first compromise."

• • •

HER WORLD HAD more than tilted. It was upside down. In thirty-six hours everything had changed. Tyler drove, leaving Santa Monica behind. They made small talk—about the carousel, laughed at being on the beach under the stars on a different coast. He held her hand across the car's console.

They kept saying in two weeks, in two weeks, in two weeks they would be together again.

So hard to say goodbye, the final quick kiss, swiping away a tear. She was at once filled with excitement over the beginning of something new, terrified at the prospect, not knowing how she was going to manage, not knowing exactly what *something new* meant.

Ty kept telling her, what was it, oh yes—we take one day at a time.

There were many unknowns, unanswered questions, swaying in the wind and neither one could foresee how they would shake out.

But one thing they did know for sure—they loved each other.

Too fast. The past hours dissolved one to the other too fast. Wanda would be at the airport to pick her up, take her back to her life at the bakery.

Buckled in her seat, the plane taxied, rose up, up, this time flying east. Star looked out the window, looked at the bright lights of Los Angeles. She strained against the seatbelt as the lights receded, as the plane climbed into the starry night. Tyler was there somewhere ... looking up at the plane, the stars. She knew he was. She pulled her short red jacket tight around her, blocking the cold air of the plane, feeling the warmth of his arms.

He promised to be home as early as possible for Christmas, the day before, or maybe two days before if he could swing it.

And, he added, "Superman keeps his promise."

Chapter 24

Dallas, Texas

LOUISE CHECKED HER WATCH, reached into her shoulder bag for her lipstick, the sticky note with the tip line number stuck to the tube. "Silly, the investigator hasn't returned my call, might as well throw the number away," she muttered. She applied the deep red lip stain, dropped the tube back into her bag, with the note still stuck to it. She'd deal with it later. Right now she was late for her appointment, a new charity needed funding, an organization to assist border guards wounded or killed in the line of duty. The meeting was only two blocks from her office. Her last patient had just left and if she hurried she wouldn't hold up the others by much.

Louise didn't flag a cab, preferring to walk, her high heeled shoes clicking on the sidewalk—faster than a cab anyway given the traffic at lunchtime.

Her cell rang and without looking at the display she answered. "Dr. Wainwright."

"Ah, finally we reach you. We've left several messages. I'm a private investigator, Manny Salinas, along with my colleague, Elizabeth Stitchway. You called the tip line, Daytona Beach Police Department, spoke with Detective Fred Watson—"

"Mr. Salinas, it was a mistake. I told the detective it was a mistake. I'm not sure why I even called. I'm also sure I don't know who your John Doe is. Now, if you will excuse me I'm late—"

"Wait, wait, Dr. Wainwright. I'm sending you a picture of John Doe."

It was a woman's voice.

"Look, Miss. … Miss.—"

"Elizabeth, Liz Stitchway. I'm Mr. Salinas's partner. Take a look at the picture, Dr. Wainwright. Then we'll stop bothering you."

A notification pinged on Louise's smart phone—a text message. Louise flicked to the message. The picture the investigator sent filled the display.

"Dr. Wainwright, Dr. Wainwright, are you there?" Liz asked.

Louise's hand began to shake. She backed against a display window, a bookstore with a display of children's books, leaned against the plate glass for support, staring at her phone. Clusters of men and women continued along the sidewalk, in a hurry, passing by the woman with a phone in her hand.

"Dr. Wainwright, this is Investigator Salinas. Do you recognize the man?"

"Yes … he's … he's my father." Her voice was barely a whisper.

"You're sure?" Liz asked.

"Yes. Dale Wainwright. My father."

"Dr. Wainwright, are you okay? This has to be a shock. Can we call someone? How can we help?"

"Where … where is he?"

"Daytona Beach morgue. Dr. Wainwright, this is Manny Salinas. We have several questions and Detective Watson can't release the body without a positive identification. Did Mr. Wainwright have a doctor? A personal physician?"

"Yes. Dr. Sandler. I'll email you his number."

"Dr. Wainwright, this is Liz again. Can you come to Florida to identify the body … answer some questions? Talk to Detective Watson so you can claim your father's body? Oh, and one more thing. Can you email us a current picture, or the latest one you have? I imagine you'd like to transport his body to Dallas for burial?"

"Yes. Of course. Where ... Orlando—"

"Orlando, or Daytona Beach. Either way, we'll meet you. Just let us know—"

"I'll arrange for a flight tonight ... with my husband. I'll send you a picture as soon as I hang up. This picture you sent ... looks like my father ... but I have to be positive—"

"Dr. Wainwright, what is your husband's name?" Manny asked.

"Jude Rattigan. I'm a psychiatrist ... kept my maiden name when we married. Hang on a minute ... okay, I just replied to your text message. My home phone and office number."

"Thanks. Got it. Dr. Wainwright, we're so sorry ... about your father. Are you sure there isn't someone you'd like us to call, to be with you?" Liz asked.

"No. I'll be all right. My husband, my daughter ... I'll call them. You said there were questions. Well, I have one. How did my father die?"

"Dr. Wainwright, that's one reason we want to talk to his doctor. We have to ascertain if he had a medical condition," Manny said

"What? A heart attack? He never mentioned anything about his heart."

"Dr. Wainwright, he may have been the victim of foul play."

Chapter 25

Daytona Beach

MANNY CLOSED HIS CELL and turned to Liz. She wasn't there. He grinned, hearing the clicking of the keys on her computer keyboard from their office.

Checking that little Lizzie was still asleep in her crib, Manny returned to the kitchen. Divvying up the last of the coffee into two mugs, he joined his wife. He loved to watch her in action. Her body language—tense, onto something juicy, right knee bouncing, barefoot heel tapping the floor. So many tidbits of information were dropped by Louise Wainwright during their conversation.

Without looking up, accepting the mug of coffee with one hand, Liz pointed to the screen with the other. "Look at this, Manny. Mr. Dale Wainwright is an oil man, or was. Must be a billionaire. A billion-billionaire. *Big* philanthropist. 'Daughter Louise, psychiatrist, represents her father in his charities.' Standard bio stuff. You call that doctor Louise told us about. She sent us an email, quick, as promised. A professional woman … must be a type *A* personality. Here, I printed the doc's number, her numbers, and email address. It's almost noon in Dallas. Maybe we can get him eating a sandwich at his desk."

"Sandwich at his desk?"

"Sure. Busy doc. Grabs a sandwich at his desk," Liz said as she punched in the number. Hit the speaker button, handing the phone to Manny. Liz turned back to her computer, tapped the keyboard entering another search.

"Dr. Sandler." The voice was that of a mature man, fiftyish.

"Dr. Sandler, my name is Manny Salinas. I'm a private investigator in Daytona Beach, Florida. My colleague, Elizabeth Stitchway, and I just spoke with the daughter of one of your patients by the name of Dale Wainwright."

"Is Dale all right? I haven't heard from him for months. I've been extremely worried … tried reaching him several times."

"Dr. Sandler, I'm sorry, but the man we believe to be Dale Wainwright is dead."

"Oh, no. I warned Dale to take care of himself, take his meds. But … you sound as if there's some question the man you're speaking about is Dale?"

"Yes and no. From what his daughter said, she recognized the man, from the picture we sent, to be her father, but she hasn't seen him yet. She's planning to fly to Daytona Beach with her husband tonight. The man we believe to be Dale Wainwright was found dead on our beach. He's been listed as a John Doe, that is until a half hour ago. We're hoping you can help in a positive identification."

"I see. I will have my staff send the coroner … this man, this John Doe is in the Daytona Beach morgue?"

"Yes. The officer in charge of the case is Detective Fred Watson. I'll email you his name, the Daytona Beach Police Department number, his cell for your records and verification as to where you're sending Mr. Wainwright's health records. Detective Watson asked me and Ms. Stitchway to investigate the case … you know, get an identification of the body and help with the cause of death—"

"The cause of death I'm sure was his cancer. Bad. Terminal. He knew he had little more than a year to live the last time I saw him. He couldn't sleep, kept on the move. He wanted to cram a lot of living into the time he had left. I prescribed something to help him sleep. He called several months back to renew the prescription. Come to think of it, he was in Florida when he called. Orlando I believe. But I'm sure my staff can tell you the drugstore location, where the medication was picked up. We generally sent his refill orders to Walgreens where he's on file so he can request a refill wherever he happens to be."

"When we talked with his daughter, she was surprised that he had been found in Daytona Beach—"

"A John Doe you said, Investigator? Surely he had identification on him."

"No. No wallet or jewelry, just his clothes. A designer label—Yohji Yamamoto."

Dr. Sandler chuckled. "That sounds like Dale. He loved Yamamoto. But, I believe he switched to another designer. Don't remember who."

Liz shrugged at Manny. John Doe was wearing another man's Yamamoto.

"By the way, it wasn't unusual for Louise not to know where her father was. They were rather estranged. She said she never knew where he laid his head on a pillow, except for the times he sent her a postcard. But then he was rather eccentric. Being a wealthy, very wealthy oil man, one can become most anything."

Chapter 26

Daytona Beach

THE FLIGHT FROM DALLAS to Daytona Beach, the two private investigators meeting the flight, the appointment with the coroner, all took place as scheduled.

Scheduled or not, when the coroner opened the body bag revealing John Doe's head and shoulders, Louise gasped, grabbed for Jude's arm. Identifying John Doe as her father, seeing his lifeless face, hit Louise Wainwright in the gut.

Louise shivered, sucked in a breath of the chlorine filled air, looked down at her father. A wave of emotion swept through her system. Her head dropped forward, eyes closed as if in prayer. Jude turned away from his wife and the corpse, as Louise raised her eyelids. Her fingers tentatively reached out, paused. She didn't touch her father's skin, instead reached higher stroking his silver streaked hair.

Her mouth open, she took a deep breath, another, and another steadying herself. Sadness slowly veiled her face—*so many years, so many wasted moments*. She loved her father. She didn't realize how deep the bond was until this moment. Too late.

Detective Watson hesitated, and then asked the question, "For the record, Dr. Wainwright, is this man your father?"

"Yes," she whispered. "This is Dale Wainwright, my father."

Jude retreated, limping to a chair by the door. His hands, fingers intertwined, rested on his stomach, feet outstretched, head against the wall, watching his wife.

Liz glanced at Manny, stepped to Louise's side laying her hand on the sleeve of her suit jacket. "Are you okay? Can I get you something? Water?"

"No. Thank you." Louise nodded to the coroner that she had seen enough, turned to leave the icy-cold chamber. Jude snapped to his feet following her back to the coroner's office.

The office seemed small with so many people circled around the coroner's desk.

"When can I take my father back to Dallas for burial?"

"You can make the arrangements to ship his body, but it will be another few days before we can release it."

"Why is that?"

Detective Watson was leaning against the wall to the side of the coroner's desk. Manny and Liz stood beside the detective. The three were watching Louise and her husband. Both travelers wore dark suits, white shirts. Louise's skirt was a tasteful inch below the knee. Jude's shirt open at the neck, no tie.

Watson answered her question. "We still can't be sure of the cause of death. We received Dr. Sandler's report, your father's health records. His cancer—"

"What cancer? I didn't know he had cancer." Louise looked to her husband, back to Watson, questioning.

"He was dying, Dr. Wainwright. From the report, the last time Dr. Sandler saw him, your father had a year, little more—which, if you count from today, would have given him a few more months. I've ordered an autopsy, pending your agreement, because from the initial blood tests and tests of what was in his stomach, there were … he had arsenic in his system."

"Arsenic?"

"Dr. Sandler's report listed a prescription for an antidepressant to help Mr. Wainwright sleep. Your father picked up a refill in Orlando three weeks before he died. From what you told Mr. Salinas, you haven't spoken to your father for awhile. Do you think he might have committed suicide? An overdose of the medication, a barbiturate, could cause death. Although we didn't find what would be considered an overdose in his system, but combined with the arsenic certainly did him in."

Louise slumped into a chair facing the desk, then stiffened her spine. "I can't imagine Dale Wainwright committing suicide. If he knew he was dying, it might explain his absences, his traveling. He embraced life, hit diversity head on ... perhaps he was traveling to places he hadn't been before. Although Daytona Beach is strange ... but Orlando ... maybe not so strange. He and my mother brought me, as a little girl, to Disney World." Her eyes welled up at the thought. *Could her father have returned to a place they visited together? Father and daughter loved that trip. Spoke of it whenever they were together ... together.*

Detective Watson broke the silence. "You can go ahead with the arrangements to transport your father the first of next week. We'll let you know the exact day. Are you okay with our proceeding with the autopsy?"

"Yes," she whispered.

Liz again stepped to Louise's side. "In the car, I mentioned a man by the name of Benny Howard. As far as we can tell, Benny was the last person to see your dad alive. He spoke with him for more than a half hour at a little bakery. It was a special occasion, the grand opening, and your father was there."

Louise looked up at Liz, her eyes questioning. "Visited a bakery? In Daytona Beach? Everything seems so strange—Florida, a bakery, arsenic, suicide?" Her voice barely a whisper, Louise shook her head unable to grasp what she was learning. "Yes. Jude and I have a return flight tomorrow morning ... I'd hoped my father would be ... yes, I'd like to meet this Benny. Wouldn't we, Jude?"

"Of course, Louise. Then, if the good investigators could take us to a hotel, I think you've had enough for one day. We can talk about the arrangements. You'll want to call your lawyer and our daughter."

"I don't know about the lawyer, but our daughter, Lou, of course. I promised Lou I'd call … after I saw the body." Louise opened her shoulder bag retrieving her business cards. Handing a card to the coroner, to Detective Watson, and the private investigators, Manny and Liz Salinas, "Here are the best numbers to reach me at—cell, office, home, and my address. Any information about my father, please call me immediately—whoever comes up with a new detail. Immediately! Now, we'd like to meet Benny."

Chapter 27

THE GROUP STRODE into Star's Bakery two-by-two—Jude a limp behind Louise, Manny and Liz. A whoosh of cool December air as the door opened and closed caused the lace window tiebacks to flutter. Wanda was helping a customer deciding which cake she wanted to buy for her dinner party—chocolate fudge or a delicate banana cream. Benny, red suspenders over his white T-shirt, sat at the cash register. Liz had called Benny letting him know that Louise wanted to meet him, the last person known to have talked to her father.

Benny looked up at Wanda. She nodded to him to go to his visitors. She would take care of the cash register.

Benny rolled up to Liz who bent over, giving him a hug. Manny in turn introduced Benny to Louise and Jude. Jude shook his hand. Louise moved to shake his hand but hugged him instead.

Benny's eyes misted as did Liz's—a couple of softies.

Benny rolled to the corner, Louise following, drawing up the chair Manny handed to her to sit beside the wheelchair. Answering a question about her flight, she leaned forward, searching Benny's eyes. "How did my father look? Did he seem to be in any kind of pain?"

"Dr. Wainwright, I'm sorry—"

"Please, call me Louise."

"Louise … I chatted with a man … we never exchanged names … chatted about the weather, had I ever been to Disney World.

Somehow he got me talking about my days with the circus. He was most attentive. Flattering it was to have such a high-class fellow interested in what I was saying."

Jude limped around the shop, stopped at the display case, bought a chocolate chip cookie, then leaned against a counter away from the others but within earshot of his wife and Benny. Liz and Manny exchanged glances, the pair always on the same wave length. They glanced back to Louise, to Jude, back to Louise. Watching. Watching.

"Benny, what made you think my father was high-class?"

"Oh, easy. He had an air about him. Not bad, mind you. Not arrogant. It was an air of a leader, educated, a man who had worked hard and achieved great things. I mean, who would wear a jacket like the one he had on unless he was comfortable with himself. Liz told me that it was a very big Japanese designer Jacket—Yamo. Or something like that."

"Did he say anything … anything about his family?"

Benny laid his calloused hand over Louise's soft manicured fingers. Even though he had a motorized wheelchair his hands remained rough from gripping the wheel. Certain places he liked to use his own power, able to keep from ramming into things.

"No, ma'am. I'm sorry. I guess, looking back, I did most of the talking. The only other thing he said besides Disney World was that he had worked in Texas, oil fields in Texas. Never said exactly where in Texas. Never said what he did. I guess you might say I was babbling … in awe of this gentleman."

While Benny was talking he kept glancing at Jude then back to Louise never losing his train of thought. Each time, his brows would knit together. Then relaxed.

"Have you ever been to Daytona Beach, Louise?"

"No. Orlando only. When my mother and father took me to Disney World."

"How, about you, Jude? Ever been here?" Benny asked looking over at Jude leaning against the display case with cakes and pies.

"Not that I recall. I'm a Texan. Worked there for Louise's father before she and I were married. Not a fond memory of the oil business."

"Why is that?" Manny asked.

Jude's attention had been on Louise, or rather Benny. He looked up sharply at Manny's question, startled that he was part of the conversation.

"I had an accident on a rig, a new hole, oil spewing everywhere. It was exciting until I almost lost my leg. Almost died."

"That must have been frightening," Liz said, glancing at her husband then back to Jude.

"You can say that again. Docs patched me up ... saved my leg. Louise, how about we head back to the hotel? It's been a long day and it'll be another one tomorrow with our early flight."

"Benny, I'm so glad I had a chance to meet you. You're very nice, and I'm sure my father enjoyed your company, his last hour as it turned out."

"I'm sorry you didn't get a chance to meet Star, the owner and brains behind Star's Bakery. She's out buying stuff for the Christmas orders."

"Maybe another time."

"Yeah, maybe another time," Benny said once again glancing at Jude as the man limped to the door.

Louise stood, moving the chair aside. "Manny, you stay. Jude and I can call for a cab—"

"Wait, you two. Benny, scoot up close to Louise and Jude so I can snap a picture with my cell. That's it ... perfect. Thanks. And Louise, don't you even think of calling a cab. Manny and I will drive you to the hotel."

Jude stood at the door holding it open for Louise, followed her out along with Manny.

Benny called out to Liz, gave the wheels a couple of mighty pushes, reached for her arm.

Liz looked down at him. "What is it, Benny?"

"That Jude fellow. I've seen him before," he whispered, his eyes darting, following Jude out the door.

"Where, Benny? He said he's never been to Daytona Beach, unless it was at one of your high-wire acts," Liz replied in a soft whisper. Benny had told her and Manny about the circus and Gigi, and how he trained on the wire to win her heart.

"No, No. I seen him. That night I talked to the man, John Doe."

"Benny—"

"I seen him plain as day. I was getting some air. All the people coming in for the grand opening ... he was crossing the street. You saw how he limps ... a handsome man like that ... limping. Something you don't forget. You tell Manny. Tell Manny, Liz. I seen him, I tell you."

Chapter 28

HER FATHER WAS DEAD.

Louise looked out the plane's window, the land morphing from one state to the other. The stewardess had given her a blanket to cover her legs. She couldn't seem to shake the chill she felt at the morgue. Leaning her head back, her hand automatically smoothed her hair back, repositioned a comb holding the French twist in place.

Cancer?

Florida? No family. No friends. His last days must have been lonely, probably painful … but to take his life? Why didn't he tell me, why didn't he let me care for him. She knew why he didn't confide, tell her he was dying … they were never close. They were once … the vacation in Florida. Disney World was such a happy time. They had been close then. After her mother died things changed. But to contemplate suicide, to commit suicide. Dale Wainwright—tough oil man? She couldn't wrap her arms around that. Arsenic? Sighing, her body trembled a moment.

Jude reached across the armrest, took her hand.

Jude. He wasn't a perfect husband. Far from it. But he was always by her side.

His fingers squeezed her hand, comforting. She squeezed in return—*thank you for being here with me, for me.*

Was that detective insinuating something more sinister than suicide? More tests? An autopsy? As a psychiatrist she had comforted patients going through death of a loved one. She'd been part of two murder cases so she knew the routine. Detective Watson suspected something. Well, she had to make plans for her father's funeral. The detective said he would release the body for transport in a few days. There would be many well-wishers.

Dale Wainwright dead!

Flowers—she'd make arrangements to have them taken to shelters, nursing homes—places where the bouquets would be welcomed, colorful bouquets of flowers to brighten their surroundings.

She would deliver a eulogy.

Dale Wainwright dead!

Why would the detective think there was foul play? Ridiculous. No one would profit from his death. I have to call Cliff Stanfield. A tear slid down her cheek thinking of her father's lawyer. They had been friends for as long as Louise could remember. I guess there's a will. Maybe he left everything to charity. God knows he had already left me financially well off. Charities will profit from his death. As they should.

His housekeeper, of course. Louise remembered the day Gladys tearfully told her how that wonderful Mr. Wainwright had set up an annuity for her.

However, her father didn't suffer fools lightly. There wouldn't be any money left to his secretary. He had fired her just before he started to travel. Found she had embezzled several thousand. No, there wouldn't be anything for her.

The plane had started its descent into the Dallas/Fort Worth International Airport. Louise handed the blanket to the stewardess, and then began a mental list of the first few calls she had to make as soon as they walked through the door of their penthouse—Lou, their daughter, then Cliff, her father's lawyer, the church, the Dallas Morning News ... and the funeral home.

Why was he in Florida? Maybe thinking of their happy vacation at Disney.

Maybe it was suicide.

Never!

Chapter 29

Daytona Beach

THE WEATHER TURNED cold over central Florida, but no frost warning for Daytona Beach. That would come sometime in January or February. Setting the grocery bags on the counter, Manny chuckled at the thought of winter. Whenever he complained about the cold to colleagues up north they scoffed. Forty-five degrees? Really? Michigan was battling icy roads, maybe a few inches of snow with a foot or more to come.

Putting the groceries away, Manny heard the clicking of a computer keyboard. He poured two glasses of wine, and joined his wife in the office. Setting their glasses on the table between their workstations, he kneaded her shoulders. Manny smiled seeing Liz's foot pumping Lizzie's rocker blade.

"Any luck? Anything interesting on Jude Rattigan?" he asked rolling a chair up next to his wife, his voice soft so he didn't disturb the baby.

"Sorta, all circumstantial. First, they have a daughter, Louise, call her Lou. Lou is married, no babies." Liz smiled at her husband. "No baby could be near as cute as our Lizzie. Anyway, Lou is a school teacher and her husband, Thomas Weed, seems to be in and out of work. Kinda like her dad, Jude. However, unlike her mother Louise, Lou took her husband's name so legally she is Lou Weed. Neither man seems to hold down a job. *Neither* of the men in Dale's family—his daughter's husband, or granddaughter's husband—seem to be motivated or just endure bad luck, like Jude with his leg. Jude, by the way, is very handsome, as we saw when we met him. He photographs like a male model. He should try it. Maybe I'll send him an anonymous tip."

"Anything in your searches show Jude in Daytona Beach? Benny certainly is positive he saw him."

"Not really, again circumstantial. Louise Wainwright is verrry involved with charities. So much so I don't see how she has time for her practice—the psychiatrist thing. I concentrated my search on the two weeks around when John Doe was found—week before and after. The Dallas Morning News features her a lot. She was traveling—ten days prior and a few days after, in Seattle at a conference on substance abuse." Liz leaned back, took a sip of wine, her brows squinched forming furrows along her forehead, mouth twitching back and forth.

"Manny, I may be trying too hard, but I found an interesting pattern. Mr. Handsome is always by her side, smiling, glad-handing—"

"That's the pattern? He's always with her?"

"Yeah, but not this time. No hubby, and no other man for that matter."

"Stitch, I had an idea while I was shopping for our dinner—roasted chicken and a salad—"

"Umm, yum. I'm starved. Mom said Lizzie was fussy yesterday but she seems to be her cute, best-baby-ever self today. I pumped some milk so I can enjoy this little treat—wine with my dinner. What was your idea?"

"Probably won't pan out, but I'm not sure how much Star has told Tyler about John Doe. I have a hard time calling him Dale Wainwright. Anyway, you know how observant the guy is, and always drawing. Why not send him a pic of John Doe?"

"Manny, it's not very flattering—dead, pasty."

"Not that one, love of my life. The one Louise sent us. The one with her father in a tuxedo. I was thinking there seems to be a connection with the bakery. Why was John Doe there? By chance?

Talking to Benny?" Manny paced a few steps, smoothing his moustache. "While you're at it, send Tyler the pic you took of Louise and Jude and Benny as they were leaving the bakery. You could say something to Tyler like ... FYI, here are John Doe's daughter and her husband."

"Ahh, no leading the witness."

"And..."

"And?" Liz said savoring another small taste of wine.

"I think I should go to Dale Wainwright's funeral. We could both go, bring Lizzie—"

"I love you, Manny, but you are fumbling ... I think *you* should go to the funeral. Lizzie and I will stay home. Your investigator women will take care of the office detail," Liz said with a smirk, her toe tapping Lizzie's rocker.

Chapter 30

Burbank, California

TYLER WAS WORKING under the gun. The first producer interested in his short-story film, The *Little Baker Girl*, had made some suggestions on how, in his opinion, the film could be improved. The producer liked the animation but asked for more emotion, more feeling from the baker girl.

Tyler was amused. The man had no idea how hot Star's feelings could run. Nonetheless, he embraced the suggestions and emailed the producer that he would have the changes back to him before Christmas. He added that he was going home for the holidays but was scheduled to return January first.

Working at his apartment, Ty sat in his Superman pajamas hunched over his computer incorporating the modifications, adding more drama pinging around in his head. He was so engrossed that he knocked over his drink of fizzy water when a ping notified him he had an email. Catching the water, the heel of his bare foot began tapping the floor in anticipation, hoping the email was from Star.

He clicked on the envelope and grinned. It wasn't from Star but was from one of his favorite subjects—Elizabeth Stitchway, Private Eye. He pictured her with her red ringlets sparking as she fed coins into the bakery's Wurlitzer, dancing to the music she selected.

Ty drew a quick cartoon of the private eye sitting at her computer, concentrating as she searched for clues, then gleefully dancing when she found a saber, the blade cutting through the air. Leaning back in his chair he swiped at the lock of hair tickling his eyebrow.

Rubbing his palms together, taking a swig of water, he read the message.

"Hi, Tyler. Miss you, and I know a certain baker girl really misses you. Manny and I are doing a little background checking on the John Doe found the night of Star's grand opening. I'm sure she mentioned it to you. Anyway, Manny and I were chatting. He thought it a good idea to send you a picture of Mr. Doe, who, by the way, has been identified as Mr. Dale Wainwright, Dallas oil man. Rich, rich, rich.

Attached are three pics. One is his daughter Louise sent us. The second is a head shot ... in the morgue (sorry, I couldn't resist), and the third I snapped when Louise and her hubby were leaving the bakery. They had flown to Daytona Beach from Dallas to ID Mr. Doe. Benny is also in that picture.

We're looking forward to your Christmas visit. Liz Stitchway, PI"

● ● ●

"Hi, Liz. Christmas! No matter how often I look at the calendar, I can still only cross off one day at a time.

Gross on the morgue pic, but yeah I did see the man in the pic you said his daughter sent. Nice looking. Very dapper. I noticed him because of his fancy duds. I saw him at the first bakeoff—you know Star's competition. He was always standing in the back. I figured him to be one of the production big-wigs. I didn't pay much attention to him— looking elsewhere as you might surmise. At the finale he sat in the back row of chairs but then moved to the back of the hall. I'll check my drawings. I think I sketched him. He was very distinctive, but come to think of it never talked to anyone. Wait, maybe he talked to Benny. And I don't remember that bozo Jim ever talking to him or standing next to him. Doe's daughter and husband look sad, stressed—that order.

Sorry, not much help. Looking forward to seeing you and that little Lizzie person. I just wish it was today. Tyler"

Chapter 31

Dallas, Texas

THE PLANE LANDED at Dallas/Fort Worth International Airport, taxied to the gate. Passengers, ignoring the flight attendant's instructions to remain buckled in their seats, began shuffling their personal items preparing to deplane.

As Manny followed along with the crowd heading to Baggage Claim, he sent Liz a quick text that he was on his way to the funeral. Liz replied: "Have news. Ty saw Doe at bakeoff. Go figure!"

Manny exited the terminal, hailing a cab to take him to the Wainwright service.

The ceremony had started so no one noticed when Manny slipped in through the open doors. The greeter handed him the biography of the oil man and the order in which colleagues, friends, and family would give tribute to his memory.

There was nothing small about Dale Wainwright's funeral.

Manny stood in the back, hands folded, head bowed in prayer. Looking up, he let his eyes rove over the three-hundred or so mourners sitting in the pews. As a whole, they looked dignified … respectful. Dale Wainwright had been cremated and the urn holding his remains was at the front, near the altar, on a small table draped with a cream-colored lace cloth. The oil-man's picture wearing a beige Stetson was framed in gold, placed to the side of the urn. In front of the picture was a nicked, smudged, white hard hat. D. Wainwright printed across the front in bold black letters.

The standing-room-only assemblage said much about the man. He was well liked, well respected, and in some cases probably feared as a relentless businessman and boss.

Louise and her husband were seated in the first pew. A young Louise-look-alike was seated on the other side of Dr. Wainwright. Manny surmised she must be Louise's daughter, Lou. And seated next to her was a man about her age, maybe the daughter's husband.

Seeing nothing out of the ordinary, nothing suspicious or noteworthy, Manny trained his eyes on the immediate family— mother and daughter and their husbands. The four knelt, prayed, sang the hymns in the order typed in the program.

Then it was over.

The internment was to be a private affair following the ceremony, following the exit of the mourners.

Louise and her daughter were dressed in black—dresses, jackets, black wide-brimmed hats, dark sunglasses, no doubt hiding Louise's red tear-stained eyes. They stood on the steps outside the church in the warm Dallas sunshine receiving hugs, blown kisses on their cheeks—everyone sorry for their loss. Manny exited the church, and along with the others was greeted by Louise who grasped hold of his arm.

"Manny, thank you for the text that you were coming. This is my daughter Louise Weed. Her husband Thom is over … over there talking to Jude. Lou this is the investigator I told you about. Still not convinced it was suicide, Manny?" she whispered.

Manny shrugged, cocked his head once to the side, said hello to Lou.

"Manny, my father's lawyer, Cliff Stanfield, asked us to come to his office tomorrow," Louise said. "Seems he wants to read my father's will as soon as possible. I'd like you to come. Here's his card with the address." Louise rummaged around in her shoulder bag, handed the card to Manny. "Eleven o'clock. You probably want to get back to Daytona Beach, but if—"

"I'll be there."

Manny nodded again to Lou and then sauntered off to a large tree, leaned back scrutinizing the family members.

Louise and Lou remained on the church steps chatting quietly with each mourner. Jude Rattigan and Thom Weed stood in an animated conversation across the expanse of lawn. Jude, black suit, white shirt, loosened his tie. Thom, black suit, sunny yellow shirt, no tie, stood with hands on his hips. Manny took the opportunity to snap a picture with his cell of mother and daughter, and several of Jude and Thom—nose to nose.

Manny was about to put his cell in his pocket when he received a text from Liz along with two attachments.

"M. Ty sent a pic he had from bakeoff. Circled Doe. Pic 2 is a sketch. Note Doe's face. Eyes on Star w fondness. Fondness? Luv U, me & little PI."

"Big PI, I will be back late tomorrow. L invited me to reading of will. Pics: Louise's daughter & her husband, Thom Weed, & Jude. Please forward all to Star. More later. Kiss little PI for me. Luv, M."

Chapter 32

CLIFF STANFIELD WASN'T looking forward to revealing to the family Dale Wainwright's recent codicil to his will. Dale Wainwright, Cliff's long-time friend and client, had executed the codicil two weeks prior to his death. Oh, it was legal—legally executed—but Cliff knew it would not sit well with Louise Wainwright and especially not with her husband.

Louise had called to apprise him that besides the immediate family members, Manny Salinas would be attending. Mr. Salinas, she explained, was a private investigator from Daytona Beach. Seemed there was still an unanswered question regarding arsenic in her father's system.

Cliff's secretary pushed the intercom button to her boss's office, informing him that the family had arrived along with a Mr. Salinas. Cliff told her to show them into the conference room, offer coffee, and he'd be with them in a few minutes. He released the intercom button, dragged his handkerchief from his pants pocket and wiped his brow. He dropped the damp cloth in his desk drawer, quickly replacing it with a fresh one from his jacket pocket.

• • •

STANFIELD'S OFFICE SUITE was sumptuous. Gleaming dark mahogany bookcases, filled with law books, lined the walls of several offices. Desks, tables, and chairs matched the rich mahogany, the cushions and backs of the chairs upholstered in a jacquard weave of maroon, navy, and slips of gold thread. Carpeting was a wine color with deep pile.

The conference room was appointed the same as the rest of the suite with the exception that only one wall carried bookcases floor to ceiling, two others were adorned with oil paintings by local artists. The remaining side of the room featured a wide expanse of windows showcasing the city, breathtaking from the twentieth floor by day, covered with white silk by night. Indirect lighting throughout the suite provided a soft glow, table and desk lamps provided direct illumination for reading voluminous legal documents.

The suite was a showcase of an established lawyer with wealthy clients.

Louise helped herself to coffee, offered to pour a cup for her daughter. Lou declined. "Lou, did you know that your grandfather had cancer? That he only had a short time to live?"

"No. Never said anything to me. Are you telling me you didn't know?"

"I didn't. It came as a shock when Detective Watson told me."

"Well, I know two men who are probably not the least bit sad that grandfather is dead," Lou whispered to her mother.

"Lou, what an awful thing to say."

"Hey, it is what it is. Thom seemed relieved. He's been pestering me for money of his own. I guess I could set something up with what Grandfather leaves to me. After all, Thom is the father of my baby."

"Lou, you're pregnant? What wonderful news." Louise wrapped her daughter in her arms.

"Yup. You're going to have a grandchild, mother."

"Finally, something happy, something to look forward to. That's why you haven't been yourself. When?"

"The doctor confirmed it a few days ago. What with your flying to the east coast, grandfather's dying, the funeral, I didn't tell you. Then with all this will stuff ... well as I said I probably should do more for Thom."

"Aside from what you said about Thom not being sad at your grandfather's death, I don't believe the same is true of Jude. As to money, I was considering doing something more for Jude. He's been dropping hints lately that he'd like additional funds in his monthly deposit. We have a pre-nuptial agreement. It's somewhat like what your grandfather urged you to execute before you and Thom were married. He didn't want either of us to have a problem with the trusts he set up for you and me. Jude's been good to me. I can't complain. You've given me a nudge. I guess I'll do something about upping his monthly sum … set up an account with stock funds of his own. Excuse me, dear. I want to have a chat with Mr. Salinas, and, Lou, I'm thrilled you're going to have a baby. We have to go shopping, fix up a nursery in that spare room of yours. A layette. Oh, sweetheart, it will be such fun." Louise hugged her daughter again.

A baby!

Lou broke from her mother's embrace, signaled she had to run to the bathroom.

"Do you want me to come with you?" Louise asked.

"No. This squeamish feeling happens. I'll be right back." Lou turned, headed out of the conference room at a fast clip.

Louise topped off her coffee, smiled at Manny gazing out at the spectacular view of the Dallas skyline. She walked across the room to speak to him.

"Thank you for coming, Manny. Cliff was so insistent that we meet today, I thought as long as you were in town you might as well learn what my father was thinking before he died … first hand."

"The funeral was moving, Dr. Wainwright."

"Please, call me Louise."

"Your father had many friends … obviously well known, well respected."

"Yes on both counts. Even though we didn't see much of each other … especially the last few years, I still miss him terribly. Wish he had confided, had let me help, but—"

"It must have been quite a shock when you called the tip-line, saw his picture—"

Louise shook her head. "Awful. I held out hope I was wrong … but when I saw him … in the morgue—"

"He never reached out to you? Especially the days surrounding his death? His depression … you'd think he would have called you."

"I wish he had. But I was away. At a conference in Seattle."

"Ahh. Jude with you?"

"No. He stayed in Texas. He's very good about escorting me to social functions, but lectures, clinical stuff bores him." Louise looked away to the door. "Finally, Cliff just came in. I'd like to get this over with. Excuse me, I have to find Lou. Let her know we're ready to start."

Louise spoke to Cliff's secretary who was laying folders at the head of the table. The secretary said a few words and Louise left the conference room.

Jude, his leg not so bad today, sauntered up to Manny, stood beside him, both men staring out the window. Jude rocked on his toes, spoke under his breath. "Mr. Salinas, I don't know why you felt you had to come to Dallas but I do know you're upsetting my wife. Her father's death, all the arrangements have been very trying. Mr. Salinas, please leave after this little conference, return to Florida, and stop badgering my wife."

Jude's tone of voice surprised Manny. He turned to reply to his accusation that he was badgering Louise, but Jude had taken a seat next to his wife, as she and their daughter had returned and were seated facing each other across the table. Manny took a seat against the wall watching the two couples—Lou and Thom Weed sitting across from Louise and Jude. Clifford Stanfield sat at the end, separating the pairs. Later, Manny described the scene to Liz saying it looked like a fighter's ring with the lawyer the referee, ready to separate the couples if needed. Except the lawyer was a small nervous man, and would probably have been trampled by the fighters.

Turned out Stanfield knew something the rest didn't and was anticipating trouble.

Clifford shuffled the folders in front of him, removed a few sheets from one, setting the papers on top. "Thank you for coming, Louise, Jude, Lou, Thom, and Mr. Salinas … at Louise's invitation." Cliff nodded to each in turn as he said their names, again wiping his brow.

"Dale Wainwright's last will and testament is straight forward, his directives short, clearly stated. Other than Louise, there is a list of people he bequeathed various sums of money to—most in the range of five thousand to ten thousand dollars. The various charities are to be managed by Louise Wainwright, named as the executor of his estate. I am named as the manager of the estate and to carry out Louise's wishes on an ongoing basis—sums of money to various charities, until the time she hires a manager or continues to retain my services."

Stanfield looked over his glasses at Louise, smiled, and sipped a glass of water his secretary had placed on the table beside the folders. "If any of you wish to see this list, my secretary will run off a copy. Louise, you will have a copy of everything we discuss at the end of the reading of the will. The original document will be retained in my office but you are welcome to examine it," Stanfield added, again looking at Louise.

"As I've already stated, Louise Wainwright, daughter of Dale Wainwright, has been named the executor of his will." Stanfield took another sip of water. Paused. Swallowed.

"Louise Wainwright is to receive twenty-five percent of the estate. Fifty percent of the total estate is to be setup in trust and administered by Louise Wainwright for the sole purpose of continuing to fund various charities, all of the charities are at her discretion—funds added to or removed from the list of donations at Louise Wainwright's sole discretion. The remaining twenty-five percent is to be used as venture capital, under Louise Wainwright's direction. Venture capital for startup oil and gas exploration, especially those companies utilizing cutting edge technology, companies that find it difficult to attract funding for their projects."

"What about me?" Lou snapped. "Aren't I mentioned?"

"You have the Trust your grandfather set up for you, Lou."

Thom jumped up. "There must be some mistake. The old man didn't even remember his granddaughter?"

"The Trust is quite large, Mr. Weed."

Jude's face tightened, fists balled in his lap. It was known to everyone, with the exception of his wife, that he despised Dale Wainwright. Blamed him for almost losing his life, almost losing his leg trying to placate her father so he would bless their marriage. As it was he ended up almost crippled refusing long operations that might have made him whole but still iffy at best. He opted instead for government disability insurance through the old man's oil company.

Thom left the table, strode to the windows. Everyone's eyes followed him except Stanfield's. Thom, breathing rapid, deep, calming himself in front of the others, returned to the table.

Stanfield reordered the folders and continued.

"Louise, your father left a personal letter for you," Cliff said, fumbling in the top folder, retrieving a sealed envelope, handing it to Louise.

Everyone sat silently as Louise slit the envelope open, her hands shaking as she spread the sheet of her father's personal stationery on the table, her eyes drinking in his words penned in his familiar handwriting.

• • •

My dear Louise, my dear dear daughter,

You're reading this letter which means I'm gone.

I'm sorry.

I'm sorry I didn't let you know that I have cancer, and I'm sorry I didn't talk to you, help you with future plans for our charities.

I beg your forgiveness, but I just couldn't stand the thought of people watching me die and saying to themselves what a poor soul, yet wishing I was already gone so they could get on with their lives.

Truth is I've had a wonderful life and have but one regret—that I buried myself in my company after your mother died.

I love you, my dear Louise. Memories of our Disney World vacation drove me to return to Florida for one last visit. Amazingly, my trip gave me a new purpose, a reason to live. I found myself caught up in the drama of a reality television show, a pilot production as it was described in the newspaper.

I wish that some day we might share a glass of wine so I can tell you of a perky blonde, a blued-eyed angel. Her ability to hit adversity head on and to triumph reminded me of you and I at our low point—the death of my beautiful wife, your mother. Your beautiful brown eyes … there are times I have to blink … I see your mother looking at me.

Dear Louise, I couldn't have asked for a better partner in fulfilling my desire to put my wealth, my good fortune, to work through charitable causes. You found the ones needing our help the most, especially our wounded warriors. Witnessing your interaction with the families—consoling, inspiring, investing in businesses they wanted to start where no one else would take a chance—was more than I dared hope for. I am proud of you as my daughter, but even more so the woman you have become.

Louise with this letter in your hand, you know there will be no sharing of a glass of wine, but also know that I wrote these words, touched the creamy linen paper to my lips with a parting kiss, and know that I love you.

Be strong, dear daughter.
Your loving father,
Dale Wainwright

• • •

LOUISE LOOKED UP to the ceiling, eyes closed.
Her father loved her!

Chapter 33

LOU AND THOM EXCHANGED GLANCES, disbelief, hatred in their eyes as to what had just transpired. They shoved their chairs back from the table. Filled with contempt, Jude also shoved his chair grasping Louise's arm, snapping her up on her feet. "Louise, let's get out of here. We have to—"

"Wait just a minute. Everyone sit down. There's a codicil to the will." Stanfield's voice was commanding, demanding them to return to their seats. His lily-white, manicured fingers fidgeted centering the knot of his tie, then smoothed his thinning gray hair back.

Louise sat. Rubbing her arm where Jude had forced her to her feet.

Jude, Lou and Thom returned to their seats. Maybe there was something for them after all.

Cliff Stanfield rearranged the green folder from the bottom to the top. He removed a piece of paper from the green folder, glanced up, eyes moving from face to face arrayed in front of him.

"Two weeks prior to his death Dale Wainwright executed this codicil in Daytona Beach, Florida. We always stayed in touch whenever he left Dallas. I attended to his needs, in particular the transfer of cash. He did not want to be found, wanted to travel to places that meant so much to him, to his late wife, and to you, Louise.

"This document was executed in front of a bank manager, wired to me, and the original with his signature sent overnight by Federal Express. The original document is in my possession and will be retained with his will. The codicil changes nothing with regard to the percentage of the total estate to Louise Wainwright, the charities, future investments, but does alter the total estate with two deductions. He bequeaths five thousand dollars to Mr. Benny Howard, and twenty-five million dollars to Miss Star Bloom, Daytona Beach. Florida."

The lawyer didn't have to wait for the eruption he was sure would come when he announced the contents of the codicil.

Jude was the first to his feet, yelling at the lawyer. "What the hell are you trying to pull, Stanfield? A bogus codicil? Louise and I will see you in court. Star Bloom? A whore, who obviously saw a mark. Wrangled money from Louise's dying father, taking advantage of his generosity. Dale wasn't only eccentric he was out of his mind, certifiably crazy."

"This time I have to agree with my husband," Louise said her voice strident. "How could this happen. That money could be used for so many causes, so many charities desperate for funding. My father would never do such a thing."

Lou ran out of the room, holding her stomach with one hand, her mouth with the other. Thom stood his ground next to Jude.

"Now wait just a minute." Stanfield had had enough. He jumped to his feet shedding his suit jacket, his tie. "Dale Wainwright executed this codicil with a clear mind. He knew what he was doing and he knew you would be upset. But, let me remind you that it was his dying wish. As for Miss Bloom wrangling, as you say, money from him, she, to my knowledge, never personally spoke with him."

"Clifford, you have to be joking," Louise stammered. She was now on her feet pacing the room. "Never spoke to her but leaves her twenty-five million? Do you think I'm stupid? Jude's right. What are you … and … and that harlot trying to pull? We will see you in court. After Christmas, I can't get away from all the fundraisers over the next two weeks, Jude and I will go to this Star

Bloom—even her name screams harlot. We'll confront her, let her know this little charade of hers, cooked up between you, *Clifford*, and my father, will never stand up in court. In the meantime, *Clifford*, carryout my father's directives in his will but hold onto that fraudulent codicil. My lawyer will be in touch with you. My new lawyer—not you, *Clifford*. I will contest the codicil to my dying breath if necessary."

"Now, Louise, don't do anything hasty." Cliff's hand was shaking as he once again reached for his handkerchief, the underarms of his shirt damp from sweat. "I've helped you and your father for decades, a trusted family confidante, trusted to carry out—"

"Trusted no more … *Mr. Stanfield*."

Jude stomped out of the conference room, slapping his good foot on the floor, pushing Lou and Thom out ahead of him. Louise yanked her shoulder bag from the floor as she turned to leave.

Manny quickly stepped forward, grasping her arm. "Dr. Wainwright, come to Florida as you just said to Mr. Stanfield. Meet Star Bloom. You'll find she's a good person and would never do what you're thinking. Call me. I'll meet your plane."

Louise jerked free of Manny's hand, shot him a look of steel as she hustled out the door.

• • •

THE ROOM WAS EMPTY but for the lawyer and the private investigator.

Manny returned to his seat, leaned his chair back against the wall, mulling over the melee that had played out in the lawyer's conference room.

Cliff Stanfield had returned to his seat at the head of the table. Drained, he leaned back, legs stretched out in front.

"Quite a bombshell, Mr. Stanfield."

"Dale knew it wouldn't sit well. I'm glad you were here, Mr. Salinas." Snapping to a sitting position, Stanfield opened the green folder retrieving an eight-by-ten manila envelope. He handed it to Manny. "There's a small sealed envelope with a letter inside, handwritten by Dale on his personal stationery. The envelope is addressed to Miss Star Bloom. Dale instructed me to make sure Miss Bloom received the letter … I don't know the contents only that Dale said he explained why he was giving the money to her. Will you deliver this to Miss Bloom for me … for Dale?"

"I'd be honored. Star Bloom is a very special friend of mine, my wife and her aunt. Star is a good person, Mr. Stanfield."

The men shook hands.

Said goodbye.

Manny rode the elevator down to the lobby of the building, strolled out into the crisp clean air. He stood next to a lamppost and sent Liz a text.

"U won't believe what just happened. See you soon. LU"

Manny shook his head. In his mind, John Doe's death had ticked up a notch closer to murder. Maybe Jude and Thom, even Louise, were more than persons of interest.

Chapter 34

JUDE THREW THE CIGARETTE butt down on the driveway, grinding it into the cement. The reading of the will swirling in his mind fanned the fury building inside of him. Charging up the front steps of his daughter's house with a hip-hop favoring his bad leg, he barged through the door, down the hall, yelling. "Lou. Thom. Where the hell are you?"

"Here, the kitchen," Thom shouted.

Jude found the pair sitting at the kitchen table, Thom's sock feet propped up on the chair next to him.

"Nice to see you too, daddy dearest," Lou said, her voice dripping with sarcasm.

Thom stood up, crossed his arms over his chest, tucking his hands under his armpits. "Things aren't going exactly like you laid out to us are they, Jude? Nothing in the will for his beloved granddaughter or her faithful husband."

Lou shot a look of warning at her husband. "Hey, watch it, Thom. Don't forget you signed a pre-nup when we got married. Grandfather insisted or he wasn't going to set up the trust … the trust that keeps us in this house and you on the golf course with your father-in-law, tootling around in that fancy cart. You and daddy dearest here make quite a pair."

"You watch your mouth, Lou." Jude stepped to her chair, raised his hand. Lou didn't flinch, knowing daddy dearest would never hit his little girl. He stepped back to the counter "Don't forget, without my suggesting to your mother she might help you with the latest remodeling, you would have taken the money out of one of your trust funds. Let's work together *children*."

"Yeah, Jude. And you're in the same boat as us, no remembrance from big-oil daddy. No thank you for all the pissy charity balls you attended with your beloved wife. And what's this about a pre-nup you and her mother signed? Were you crazy?"

"What you don't know is the pre-nup I signed, to get the holier-than-thou oil man's blessing, is no longer in effect. After twenty years, the document is null and void. Not sure if your mother remembers that little clause, Lou. Texas is a no-fault state in case of divorce. The parties, split fifty fifty."

"I'm pregnant, Daddy. Thom and I—"

"What?"

"I said, I'm pregnant."

"Hell of a time. Does your mother know?"

"I told her before the meeting with Cliff started. It all makes me sick ... literally," Lou said stroking her belly.

"Well, maybe we can use your announcement. How did Louise take the news?"

"Overjoyed!"

"Yeah, well ..." Jude, his feet slapping the floor as he paced over the slate tiles of the kitchen, copied from a design highlighted in the Architectural Digest. He stopped, turned to his daughter. "How are you feeling? When's the baby due?"

"Horrible. Mid-July."

"A baby could change everything. We have to sit tight. One idea, Lou. You should volunteer to help your mother, help her manage the millions slotted for Dale's charities.

"Umm, the dutiful daughter volunteers to help her mummy?"

"Yes, especially help with the dispersal of funds to the charities, with Cliff's help, of course. Now, don't either of you do anything stupid, watch your mouths. We'll keep quiet until Louise meets the bimbo. When she returns to contest the will, we'll lobby for other changes at the same time or we'll threaten repercussions?"

"Like what, Daddy?"

"I have a few ideas?"

● ● ●

IT HAD BEEN A TRYING two days to say the least—her father's funeral, then this awful Will business. Louise had spent the day in her office with patients and arrangements for charity events scheduled during the holidays. She looked at her image in the mirror of her vanity. The years had been kind to her. Thanks to her father she lived in the upper-crust of Dallas society with her handsome husband. She removed the combs holding her hair in place, releasing the auburn waves to her shoulders.

Something was niggling around the edges of her mind. What? The meeting with Cliff had been very unsettling … no, it wasn't that. She had learned from her daughter that she was pregnant. That was wonderful news.

She let her delicate peach peignoir slide off her shoulders as she brushed her hair, sipped the wine in the crystal goblet. Her nightly ritual—a little wine while she brushed her hair waiting for Jude to join her in their bed.

Lou had mentioned Thom was asking her again for a little more money in her monthly deposit into his account. Louise told her that Jude had said something of the same thing. Jude. He was always attentive even though their pre-nup was no longer an issue. She had told her father that it was no longer necessary. Yes, she'd look at all the finances after the first of the year, make some changes.

Louise wasn't sure if Jude recalled the date their pre-nup would be void. She saw no reason to bring it up.

A new lawyer? No, she had been upset with Cliff. Dear Cliff. So faithful to her father. No, she wouldn't seek a new lawyer.

Louise tilted, turned her arm, the reflection in the mirror showing a bruise. Her fingers touched the black and blue spot. A little sore.

Jude walked up behind her, put his arms around her, kissed the back of her head. He saw the bruise, kissed it. "There, all better, sweetheart."

She smiled up at him, their reflection. They made a handsome couple.

Chapter 35

MANNY WALKED IN the backdoor to a raucous homecoming. Maggie and Peaches sat expectantly in front of their master, tails sweeping the floor, muzzles nudging his thighs. Liz handed him a large mug of coffee, lid clamped down tight. Lizzie was sucking on the nipple of a small bottle of water looking at her daddy with her big brown eyes, legs kicking in greeting as Liz strapped the baby into her carrier.

What a homecoming. He loved every minute of it. "I take it we're going somewhere?" Manny said.

"You've got that right. The bakery."

"You do realize it's after ten o'clock—the stars are out not the sun, my love." He titled her chin up for a quick kiss.

"Umm … I like that. I called Star about the pics you asked me to forward to her. She said to come to the bakery whenever. She and Gran are frosting a big order of Christmas cookies. Don't worry, that coffee will perk you right up. After I forwarded all the pics you sent to me, she replied to come to the bakery pronto. Well, she didn't say pronto. She said as soon as you got back. Same thing."

Liz gave each dog a bone telling them they were now on guard duty, and jogged to the car. Manny buckled Lizzie in the backseat, hustled back to his car. He grabbed his briefcase, tossed it on the seat next to Lizzie along with a kiss on her mop of red curls.

On the way to the bakery, he related to Liz what he witnessed at the funeral and at the reading of the will, but stayed clear of his thoughts on the pictures. He wanted her reaction along with Star's, but wanted their fresh perspective, not an annotated version taking into account his comments on the situation. That would come later.

The bakery was lit up—little white lights framing the picture windows. Three two-foot white Christmas trees with colored lights were centered in each window. A black and white closed sign hung on the front door.

"Star said to come around back, knock three times so she knows it's us. We don't want to scare them."

"You knock, I'll bring Lizzie. Good heavens, I think she's grown and I've only been gone two days. We have to set up her college fund."

"Really, Manny, I think we have a few days before we have to worry about that."

The backdoor swung open sending a strip of light across the pavement. Star hugged Liz, a squeeze on Manny's free arm. "How about setting Lizzie over by the flour bin? Manny, I've seen that Thom guy."

"Mary, nice to see you," Liz said. "These cookies are very pretty."

"Hello, Manny," Gran said. "Here, both of you have a cookie. There's fresh coffee."

"Thanks, Mary." Manny set Lizzie as directed, then fished out his cell bringing up the pictures he snapped at the funeral. "Wait a minute. Star, did I hear you right? You just said you saw this guy? I snapped the picture thinking it was a long shot. It's Lou's husband, Louise's son-in-law. He took off his jacket as he got into the limo – leaving the funeral with the family. You've seen him? Where?"

"I didn't recognize them in the first picture—remember I was not here when you and Liz brought Louise and her husband to the bakery to talk to Benny. But the last picture, the man getting in the long black limo, the tattoo. I remember thinking how sweet that was—the heart with Lou inside. See, I thought the name Lou was probably a partner, not a wife in the conventional way. I saw him in Costco, the line over at the next checkout. I don't know what he was buying."

"And you didn't recognize the pics of Louise and Jude because you didn't meet them."

"Right. But what does the guy with the tattoo have to do with John Doe? I know, I know. I'll stop calling him that. Liz told me his name is Dale Wainwright. I'm pretty sure I've never seen him either. The picture you sent—"

"Star, why do you say you're pretty sure?" Liz asked.

"I don't know. I've seen so many people—the diner, the competition. I never really focused on anyone's face unless I knew them."

"Star, my trip was very interesting to say the least. Cliff Stanfield, he was Dale Wainwright's lawyer, insisted the reading of his Will take place the day after the funeral."

"Why did he insist? From what I've read in the newspaper it can be done days, weeks, months after a funeral service," Star asked handing Gran another bottle of green food coloring.

"He had information that he knew was not going to sit well with the family, and that dear friend is where you come in. When Liz hustled me out the door tonight, I didn't complain because I wanted to see you."

"Me? Why would my name come up?"

"Just a second, I have to get my briefcase." Manny ran out, the eyes of the women following him. Running back in, he closed the door, set his briefcase on the floor next to Lizzie. He retrieved a cream colored envelope from his case, lifted Lizzie's little hand to his lips. She jerked at the intrusion on her dreams.

Grinning at Liz, her eyes wide, a slight shake of the head, warning him not to wake the baby. Manny straightened up, handed the envelope to Star. "I don't know what this letter says. Read it. Maybe it will give you some answers ... maybe I can fill in some blanks."

Star took the letter from Manny and, with a sharp knife, slit the envelope open. Her eyes began tracing the words handwritten on the creamy stationery.

• • •

My dear Miss Bloom, Star, please forgive me for being so forward, calling you Star. I feel I know you personally.

Let me explain.

My journey with you started on a visit to Disney World where I saw a newspaper article, an announcement of an Amateur Bakeoff competition. I was feeling poorly, a bit down that day, and thought this might be something to bring me out of my depression.

And, oh my, there you were, a contestant in the bakeoff, held in a rundown building in Daytona Beach. I quietly delved into your personal story, picking up bits and pieces about you from the producers. And, I learned more as you remained in the competition, never one to be sent home at the end of that particular episode. Between episodes, your admirers answered my questions telling me more about you.

Please forgive my intrusion. I saw my daughter in you—tough, always picking yourself up, pushing forward, yet soft and feminine on the inside.

I snuck into the hall and watched you compete in every episode being filmed. One day as you sat on the floor watching your pie crust through the oven window, I was reminded of the first hole I drilled for oil.

What a day that was for me and my crew. I listened and watched the oil rig, drilling and drilling, boring deeper and deeper into the ground, waiting and waiting always asking, will I strike oil today? They called us wildcatters.

My dear, Star, I did strike oil that day—she spewed sky high out of the ground falling back to earth dowsing me and my men with her rich, black gold. Forgive my rambling. You see several months ago I had been diagnosed with inoperable cancer. Watching you eased my pain—you will never know how taking part in your struggle, from afar, I was young again, looking forward to each day. You see, I had a dream once, but no funds to bring it to life. I sought investors. They all said no, except one. I trust I can be that one for you. The thought brings a smile to my lips, peace to my heart.

You didn't notice me at the bakeoff. You never saw me, but I was there every episode. When you won the competition I was cheering with the rest of those following you.

I watched you steer a man in a wheelchair to your baking station in that final episode. I asked the person sitting next to me about the man. As the story went, you rescued him the first time you entered the diner. Seems his wheelchair was at cross purposes with the door. Thereafter you treated him as a special friend and he obviously overcame any discomfort he felt so he could wish you good luck, be in attendance for the last episode. His story only added to my respect for you.

But when I read the next day, not of your victory and winning the prize money, but of the scoundrels slinking out of town, I sunk back into a deep depression.

But then a few days later, I went to the diner where I was told you worked, but you were not there that morning. I saw a cartoon of you on the wall of the diner, and another on the back of a paper placemat. The cartoon was a baker girl smiling out at me, her twinkling eyes full of hope.

That's when I decided to step in to help soften the blow of losing the prize money after winning the competition. Later that day I left an envelope for you, tucked next to the cash register at the diner. A promissory note for a hundred thousand dollars.

You made me laugh when I saw the diner close and you, not missing a beat turning right around and opening a bakery a few blocks away, with the name of *Star's Bakery* over the door.

We may never meet, but I want you to know what a strong young woman you are and that nothing will hold you back from a wonderful, fulfilling life. Never hesitate to take a risk that in your heart you believe in, if only you had the nerve. Go for it, Star, like you did at the bakeoff competition. Like your plans for a bakery. Do this and your life will be filled with one adventure after another.

My dear Star, if you're reading this letter, it means you will soon receive another gift from me—twenty-five million dollars. It gives me great pleasure to leave this very small piece of my estate to you in thanks for helping me through a difficult time, for helping to relieve my pain. Thank you, dear Star Bloom.

Your friend,

Dale Wainwright.

PS: Please give Benny Howard the enclosed check for $5000. Our long conversation at the bakeoff when you won the competition added to my faith in the human spirit to overcome adversity, adversity that Mr. Howard faces every day.

• • •

STAR SLUMPED ONTO A STOOL beside the counter in the center of the kitchen where all the mixing, sifting, icing took place. She put the check for Benny in her pocket and handed the letter to Gran. Wiping her hands on her apron, she took the letter from Star's fingers.

Silence filled the bakery's kitchen as Gran read the letter. Liz had no idea what was in the letter, must have been very bad news from Star's reaction.

Looking at Manny, Star slowly shook her head. "I don't believe it. Twenty-five million dollars. Did you know?"

Liz let out a gasp ... *twenty-five mil?*

"Yes. I knew," Manny said. "Louise Wainwright invited me to attend the reading of her father's will. Dale Wainwright drew up a codicil to his will, leaving that sum of money to you. No one knew about the codicil, except his lawyer. It came as quite a shock. Star, that's the good news. The bad news is that the family—his daughter, granddaughter and their husbands are very upset. So upset, in fact that Louise and her husband are coming here to meet you. She wants to size you up, called you some very unpleasant names, swears she will have the codicil overturned, set aside."

"When is she coming?"

"Not sure. A day or two after Christmas. I think she'll call me because I told her that you are not the monster she was making you out to be. I told her I'd pick her up at the airport."

Gran handed the letter to Manny to read, Liz reading it over his shoulder.

Manny then handed the letter back to Star. "A word of warning, she's coming here thinking you seduced her father, coming to accuse you of wrangling money from him. I think Louise Wainwright might change her mind if she reads her father's letter to you. Put it in a safe place, like a safety deposit box at the bank. The letter will stand as proof that you never met him. Make a copy to show Louise when she arrives."

"Wow, he was at the bakeoff ... every episode." Star shook her head, looked at Gran, both unable to comprehend the life-changing magnitude of what Mr. Wainwright wrote in the letter.

"Maybe that's why I hesitated, just a moment, when you asked if I had seen the man in the picture. Everything was always so chaotic, stressful at the bakeoff, my eyes could have glanced his way but my brain didn't register him."

Manny took out his phone again, thumbed through the pictures to the one Louise had sent with her father in a Tuxedo. "Here, look at this from his daughter. I guess they were at a charity ball."

Star took his phone, looked at the picture, then up at Manny. "Benny. This is the man Benny was talking to at the opening. I remember because of his bow tie ... Tyler wore a black bow tie everyday at the diner. I remember wishing Tyler was at my opening. Of course, that was before Superman strolled through the door," she added giggling.

Chapter 36

The Day Before Christmas

IT WAS ALL HANDS ON DECK.

Dressed in their uniforms—black shirt embroidered with Star's Bakery, black slacks, a white frilly apron floating over all, the bakers set to work for the final push. Everyone arrived at 5:00 a.m. except for Benny who kept to his routine—coffee, newspaper, cash register at 9:00 a.m. Star braided her hair into little piglets keeping it out of her eyes and off her neck. Today was going to be a barn-burner but she was ready.

Everyone staked out their territory on the kitchen's long center island. The Butterworth sisters took command of one end—Hattie and Mattie one side, Anne the other. Wanda bustled in the back door muttering that she was sorry she was late, joining Anne across from her sisters.

The sisters and Wanda were in charge of bread, cake and piecrusts—anything to do with flour. Pie crust shells, navy beans covering the golden unbaked dough to prevent a soggy bottom, were baked. Hattie retrieved the crusts from the oven, sliding the perfect bottom crusts to Gran. She took over with the fillings and necessary top—dough crisscrossed, completely covered, or not—popping the pie into the oven for the final baking.

Gran and Star labored on either side of the remaining three-foot wide section of the island finishing the pies and mixing, baking, and frosting cookies with or without sprinkles.

Gran and Star kept exchanging glances—twenty-five million darts shooting between them. Star swore Gran to secrecy—the late-night meeting with Manny and Liz. However, the sisters knew something happened when Mattie found a bootie, a pink bootie, on the floor in front of the shelf with the flour bin. A little *L* was appliquéd on the side. That moppet Lizzie had paid a visit. Mattie handed the bootie to Star who merely said thank you and that she would see to it that the bootie was returned to Liz.

Once the bakery opened the ka-ching of the register rang out merrily non-stop. Benny was decked out with new red suspenders over a new red and green plaid shirt, unbuttoned to reveal his white Star's Bakery Tee. Grinning, he thanked the customers, wishing them a merry Christmas or a happy holiday, as he rang up the sale.

Two culinary-art students filled in for the better part of the day, bagging and boxing the orders for pickup, dashing back and forth between the front of the shop and the kitchen when Star or Gran called out that a pie, cake, or whatever was ready.

The Wurlitzer played holiday music nonstop including *I'm Dreaming of a White Christmas*, thanks to Benny, who also added a spritz of fresh snow to the front windows. Star saw her opportunity to talk to Benny quietly as he stood back admiring the new snowfall.

"Benny, I can't explain right now, but I have check that's burning a hole in my pocket."

"Aw, Star, we all agreed no gifts—"

"This isn't from me. It's … well, it's from a friend of yours, Dale Wainwright."

"But I didn't know him, we talked, but we didn't exchange names."

"I know, but you made quite an impression. He wrote me a letter before he died. He asked me to give this to you with his words ... Benny Howard faces adversity every day." Star retrieved the folded check from her pocket, handing it to Benny.

Unfolding the check, his brows furrowed at the amount. "This is a lot of money ... more than I ever ... is it real?"

"I'm pretty sure it is. As I said, I'll tell you more later. You're a special, wonderful person, Benny. Merry Christmas." Star kissed his check. Feeling her eyes mist, she turned, quickly walked back to the kitchen.

At 3:26 p.m., thirty-four minutes before closing, everything came to a halt. Superman strolled in completely undoing Star.

The final pickup-orders left the shop, customers hugging everyone, the staff hugging each other and anyone else who walked within range. Holiday greetings, kisses on cheeks, pumped up the celebration as the hands on the clock swung to closing time.

Wanda shut the front door, turning the swinging sign from *Open* to Closed. Per Star's direction, Wanda tucked a twenty dollar bill into the envelopes with the student's pay. Wanda also put out the offer to Gran that she'd give her a ride home given Superman was lingering around a certain baker girl. The offer was accepted. Gran picked up a fresh loaf of sour dough, commenting that a tuna sandwich and a glass of wine were in her future, and a long sleep, after a long day. Superman reminded Gran that she and Star were invited to the Jackman's for Christmas dinner. He would be around to pick them both up at noon tomorrow.

The sisters made their exit with Benny, after a final round of hugs calling out that they would see them in two days. Wanda and Star had decided that a two-day holiday was due everyone. Wanda paused a few minutes asking Tyler about California and how he liked his job, then she and Gran said goodbye.

Benny had fed the Wurly with several coins before leaving with the sisters, so holiday music continued to fill the little bakery as Star turned off the shop lights, pulling Tyler into the kitchen.

Star leaned in as Superman circled the blonde baker girl with pigtails into his arms.

The white lights twined around the shop windows twinkled merrily along with the soft colored lights dancing from the Wurly.

The magic of Christmas Eve settled into Star's Bakery on Atlantic Avenue.

Chapter 37

Christmas Eve

RELUCTANTLY, THEIR EMBRACE ENDED.

Superman leaned back, gazed into the baker girl's big blue eyes. "I love you, star of mine. I've missed you," he murmured playfully fingering a piglet.

"Oh … you have no idea."

"How about dinner? You must be starved."

Star sighed. "I'd love it. But where? I have something big to tell you and a restaurant isn't—"

"Not a problem, Miss Bloom. Superman has the menu under control. He most assuredly stocked his refrigerator with a roasted chicken, a side of salad, and that chocolate fudge cake I saw. The last one, I might add, in your display case will top dinner off nicely … don't you think?"

"I think!" Star said, her lips smiling. "Here's a box. You get the cake while I close up." Star locked the bakery's back door, turned out the light, stepped through the swinging door and into Superman's second embrace. A thought mingled with the electric shot … *how nicely their bodies melted together.*

Driving to his parent's home, he kept hold of her hand, raising it time and again to his lips.

His studio apartment, over his parent's three-car garage, glowed softly with indirect lighting as they entered. Once again he pulled Star into his arms.

Another long embrace.

Letting his arms fall to his side, he smiled, his right hand grazing her cheek. "There's a bottle of white wine in the fridge. Glasses on the counter. Can you pour us a glass while I change into Tyler Jackman?"

"I think I can manage that although I kinda like the goose bumps coming from Superman's kisses." They both laughed as he stepped away to the walk-in closet at the end of the studio, bordering the futon sleeping area. Star turned to the galley kitchen and the wine assignment. She took a minute to pull the elastics from the pigtails, freeing her hair to soft wavy curls falling to her shoulders.

Returning, Ty picked up his glass, arms around her shoulders guiding her to the buttery soft leather couch facing the computer work area across the way. Above the computer monitor was a wall mounted television he used to scrutinize his animations for editing.

A sip of wine, a kiss, the cuddling on the couch quickly turned into a desire to quench their thirst, not for the wine but for each other. Throw pillows on the thick red Oriental rug, their hearts beating faster, and faster to the rhythm of the music emanating from the sound system Tyler had flicked on when they entered his private space. The hunger from the two week separation flamed, until their thirst for each other was quenched and they lay sated in each other's arms, the racing blood slowly returning to normal.

● ● ●

TYLER, HIS HEAD ON A PILLOW, Star's arm circled his chest. Touching one of her wavy curls tucked under his chin, he stared at the pine paneled ceiling. *So this is what love feels like.*

"I believe Superman said something about a roasted chicken," Star whispered nestling tighter into the crook of his arm.

"He has a big mouth … but, I believe he was right. Of course, we could start with the fudge cake." Tyler slowly sat up, smacked a kiss on her forehead. "Wait here … I believe Superman hung two cozy robes in my closet."

"Umm … he certainly is thoughtful."

"Always, Miss Bloom."

Returning with two thick white terrycloth robes, he helped Star to her feet, wrapping her in a robe along with an embrace.

"I'll put the salad out—buffet like," Star said pulling him to the counter framing the galley kitchen.

"Very well, mademoiselle, I shall attend to the bird. More wine?"

"Yes, please."

Star lit the three candles on the black granite counter, their flicker casting homey soft shadows.

Helping themselves to salad and pieces of chicken, they quickly perched on the counter stools. Tyler had retrieved their wine glasses from the floor in front of the couch, barely touched, topping them off. "To a wonderful Christmas," he said raising his glass to hers.

"To a promise kept … returning home for Christmas," she said raising her glass to him.

"I believe you told Superman you had some big news. Since he left, can you tell me?"

Star put her fork down, took a sip of wine and turned to Ty sitting inches from her. She put a hand on his raised knee, his foot on the middle rung of her stool.

"You know all that business with the body, with John Doe, the pictures forwarded back and forth between Manny and Liz, and you and me?"

"Yeah. Has the mystery of his death been solved? I guess they've identified him?"

"Dale Wainwright. A big oilman. A very big oilman. Ty … I don't even know how to tell you. Wait, I have a copy of the letter in my shoulder bag. Let me get it. The letter will explain way better than I can."

Star slipped off the stool.

Ty added a touch more wine to their glasses.

Perched back on the stool, Star handed Tyler a white business-size envelope.

He glanced at her. A quick peck on her lips. He opened the envelope and began to read the letter.

Tyler slid off the stool, read it again as he circled the counter. "Am I reading this right? Dale Wainwright left you twenty-five million dollars?"

Star's face was serious as she nodded. "But wait. Manny said it will be contested. Mr. Wainwright's family, well his daughter, is furious. She thinks I seduced her father into giving me the money. Those were her words, Manny said, plus some others he wouldn't repeat."

"Does Manny think she'll prevail?"

"He doesn't think so, mainly because of this letter. Gran and I went to the bank, opened up a safety deposit box. The original of the letter and the envelope are in the box."

"My God, Star, what are you going to do?"

"Nothing. I can't do anything until the matter is settled. Manny evidently talked to Louise Wainwright about coming to Daytona Beach to meet me. He told her I was a good person, so her father knew what he was doing."

"And, are they coming?"

"Yes, day after Christmas ... or the next. Ty can you be with me when they come? Your last text ... you thought you might have to return to Burbank before New Years."

"No ... yes, I did say that. But I told the company I couldn't possibly be back until January first or second. I told them I had serious business to attend to."

Tyler folded the slip of paper returning it to the envelope.

"Serious business? Everything okay with your parents?"

"You, Miss Bloom, are my serious business. This letter ... it changes things." Tyler looked at Star, his face veiled with apprehension.

Chapter 38

Christmas Day

STAR HAD CALLED Cindy asking what she was planning to wear for the Christmas celebration. The two giggled as the dress code morphed from comfy casual jeans to long gowns and sparkly jewels to a happy medium of cocktail dresses—long, short, or somewhere in between.

Gran was thrilled. She hadn't had an occasion to wear her black A-line short sleeved dress with a modest scoop neck. She had purchased the dress in New York City, bedazzled by the dress's embellished rhinestone buckle.

Dressing for the evening, Star was in heaven peeling off her jeans, T-shirt, and sneakers, soaking in a hot tub. Gran threw in a handful of bubble bath salts before Star stepped in to the bubbles erupting around her.

• • •

THE SETTING WAS PERFECT—a movie set.

The flickering candles down the center of the dining room table covered with a white damask cloth, added to the flames crackling in the corner fireplace, sending rainbow sparks of light off the chandelier's crystal droplets, off the crystal wine goblets. Colored lights twinkling against the glass ornaments on the tree in the foyer were visible through the dining room arch.

Tony, Tyler's dad, stood at the head of the table carving the golden brown turkey. Cindy, Tyler's mom, had removed the extra leaves of the table creating an intimate family gathering.

Gran and Star sat on one side of the table, Tyler the opposite side, host and hostess completing the circle on either end.

Tyler and his dad doffed their blazers when Tony began the carving, Tyler standing by his side holding the platter to receive the succulent slices of turkey. It was a good thing all he had to do was stand there because he couldn't tear his eyes away from Star. The midnight-blue intricate lace overlaying a form-fitting sleeveless sheath, lustrous satin outlining the scoop neck, captivated him. Star was way more beautiful than any woman in Hollywood.

Cindy was the picture of a perfect hostess in a silvery gray lace—V-neck, fluttery short sleeves. Her dark brown hair pulled back into a chignon revealed a pair of sparkling diamond earrings—a gift from her husband.

Chatter, soft laughter mingled in the air with the scent of roasted turkey, as Tyler related stories of his group sessions over the characters he and his colleagues were creating, giving form, emotion, and voice to their antics. He didn't mention California but did exchange a smile with Star, a smile that was not lost on his parents.

Gran told stories of how she and Star worked in the kitchen together preparing family feasts on Thanksgiving—all of the holidays.

Anyone peeking in the window would have seen a family enjoying each other on a special occasion.

Of course, everyone around the table was aware of Star's gift from John Doe. Tyler had told his folks that morning sitting at the kitchen counter while his mother stuffed the turkey, father and son sipping coffee. The housekeeper had the day off, leaving the Jackman home the day before around noon to join her family in Orlando. The baking, setting the table, last minute flower arrangements finished, Cindy scooted her out the door with a hug, wishing her safe travel and to enjoy being with her sister and family.

Everyone also knew that Mr. Wainwright's daughter and her husband were arriving the next day around noon from Dallas to meet with Star, meet with Star to accuse her of seducing her father. They all knew but never spoke of it. Manny had called Star that morning confirming their arrival. Tomorrow was tomorrow and today was Christmas.

After the feast they adjourned to the little theater Tony designed, cabled to Tyler's computer in his studio over the garage. Tonight's attraction, while sipping an espresso laced with Grand Marnier—a preview of *The Little Baker Girl*. The short animation production Tyler sent to a producer, the producer who had shown interest but, as of yet, had not offered a contract. The three elders sat in the first row, each chair upholstered in soft black leather, a cup and small plate holder attached to the arms held the coffees. Star and Tyler sat in the second row, Tyler's arm across the two consoles holding Star's hand. Neither mentioned Star on the carousel's white horse, Tyler standing close, hand up to hers.

Cheers, applause, praise were heaped on Tyler along with a standing ovation. Everyone agreed it was a winner no matter what happened. Cindy suggested he enter it in the animated film category at the Cannes film festival next May.

Settling back in their seats, Tyler dimmed the houselights for the feature film Cindy selected for the evening—*It's a Wonderful Life* with Jimmy Stewart and his struggles as George Bailey.

The celebration wound down after the movie, conversation spent. It had been agreed that an exchange of presents was not in order—it was enough to be together. Cindy, however, tucked an aged bottle of Port wine under Gran's arm. She thought perhaps Gran and Star might like to imbibe before turning out the light. With hugs, kisses, and promises to return soon, Tyler settled Gran and Star in the backseat of his mom's car, waved his limo-driver cap, rented along with Superman's cape and tights, to Tony and

Cindy as he drove out of the driveway and on to Star's studio apartment.

Tyler gave Gran a hand as she exited the car scooting to the front door. Star whispered to her that she'd be right in and to pour a cordial of the Port for both of them.

Tyler turned Star into his arms, holding her, protecting her from what was to come.

Her arms circled tightly around him as well, her head on his chest nestled under his chin. "Thanks for a wonderful Christmas, Ty. Your mom and dad were so thoughtful, welcoming Gran and me."

Ty lifted her chin. Her eyes, brows drawn tight. She was apprehensive over what tomorrow might bring. "Don't worry, Miss Bloom. I'll be with you. And if they're mean, Superman will drive them away."

Chapter 39

A SCRAGGLY TWO-FOOT Christmas tree that Star saved from the scrapheap, sparkled brightly in the corner, adorned with a string of colored lights. The needles, sparse as they were, filled the small space with a faint aroma of pine.

Gran and Star huddled side-by-side on the bottom bunk, each wrapped in a blanket, sipping a cordial of the Port wine Cindy gave to Gran. A candle flickered on the little table next to the futon couch.

Star leaned back against the wall, ducking her head so she didn't smack the bunk above. "I'm glad I called Mom and Dad this morning, wishing them a merry Christmas. It seems forever since I've seen them … almost a year … almost a year since I came to Daytona Beach. Gran, did you miss being with the family today?"

Gran chuckled. "Star, there are so many twists and turns going on around here I don't have time to miss anyone … maybe a little."

"Did you have a nice time with the Jackmans?"

"Hard not to have a good time. They are wonderful people. They seemed to like the basket we put together. Did you see Cindy's eyes? The bread and pies will do nicely with Tyler being home."

"She was more than happy with the Christmas cookies you wrapped to give to friends who drop by this week for some holiday cheer. And, of course, the little bundles of taffy. I still can't believe we had time to make the taffy for the holidays. Hattie and Mattie stepped up big time. Some customers bought the whole jar—not just a little bag. Oh, and the chocolate-fudge brownies. Anything fudgy is a winner in Ty's book."

"How about you, dear? Did you have a good time?"

"Oh, yes. How about their theater?"

"Star … Tyler loves you … you know that don't you?"

"Yes, I know. Gran … what's going to happen? What am I going to do?"

"Take one day at a time, sweetie. Don't borrow trouble. You don't know about this Louise Wainwright. You show her the letter … well, surely she'll come around."

"I don't know. Gran, I'm in love with Ty. We're good together."

"That boy makes me laugh. His film of the Little Baker Girl is precious. You both have a lot to think about. Big decisions. He seems to be ensconced in Burbank. You here on the East Coast. I'm not in favor of commuting relationships. Twenty-five million … so much money. You could do so…..so, well a lot with it … set up quite a life for the two of you–east coast … west coast."

"But, Gran, I just opened a bakery. People are depending on me—you, Wanda, and Benny. I have a new life because of the bakery. And then the Butterworth sisters. How can I leave them? Quit so soon? What kind of a person is that? I dreamed of a bakery since I was little."

"Star, dreams when you are a little girl change. You may have outgrown, or rather you may be ready to take what you've learned and add to it—you've talked about a cookbook for children, an interactive E-book, you said. And, I guess we know someone who could help with that. Oh my, Tyler would run with your idea. You two would be a regular corporation."

Star giggled, scooched off the lower bunk for the bottle of Port, paused. "Gran would you like half a turkey sandwich? Cindy gave me some slices."

"Yes, I would, dear. But just half. And maybe switch to seltzer water. I don't want to have a hangover tomorrow."

Star began to laugh. Stopped. Gran was right. She had to be clear headed tomorrow. "There are so many irons in the fire as Dad would say. My interview with Mr. Roth—is he going to offer some kind of job? And then there's Ty—what if his short film is accepted and they want him to create others?" Star shook the thoughts from her head. "Anyway, I'm glad we called the family this morning."

Star brought a small plate with the turkey sandwich cut on the diagonal, and two sturdy mugs of seltzer so they wouldn't tip on the bed.

"Yes, they sounded well. I worry a little about your father. He works so hard. Umm, I didn't think I'd ever eat again, but this turkey with our crusty olive loaf is wonderful."

"We do bake spectacular bread, Gran."

"Dear, I've wanted to tell you something, and now with all your planning, I think the time is right. The schedule at the bakery is a bit much for me. I've been thinking, seriously this time, of going home to Hoboken. Hearing your father's voice today … well, maybe it's time. I've been here with you now for almost six months. I never intended to stay that long … but my, it has been fun."

"Gran, you've been wonderful. I've taken advantage of you … I'm so sorry. I can't imagine going through all this without you."

Gran patted Star's hand. "Nonsense, child. I've done exactly what I wanted to do every hour. But the last few days … well, I think they were a harbinger of the level of activity that is required to keep a full-fledged bakery going. And, Star dear, your bakery has quickly become a fixture on the strip. You should have heard Benny talking to the Butterworth girls—mercy me. They had you expanding to deliver fresh baked goods to the local markets. Anyway, let's see what the next few days hold. Keep an open mind."

Picking up the empty plate and their empty mugs, Star padded to the dishwasher. "You're right. And, I think we'd better get some sleep. Can I get you anything before I climb up the ladder?"

"I'm fine, dear. Thank you for a most wonderful Christmas. I love you."

"Love you too, Gran. Goodnight."

Star blew out the candle, turned off the tree lights and climbed up to the top bunk pulling the covers up under her chin. Her thoughts were winding down, but one persisted, Dale Wainwright's words. *Never hesitate to take a risk that in your heart you believe in, if only you had the nerve. Go for it!*

Chapter 40

Dallas, Texas

THE CHARITIES NEEDED her attention with year-end tax issues, and the hue and cry for additional funding had risen to a fever pitch. What was she doing, leaving town to confront a predator, a predator who succeeded in getting into her father's generous heart.

Swearing, muttering under her breath, Louise yanked her large tote from the back of the closet. She was furious at the lawyer, furious at Manny Salinas for suggesting she fly to Florida see for herself, to meet, to take stock of the person who swindled her father's estate out of millions that could have gone to charity. But most of all she was furious with herself for taking the bait.

What could the trip possibly prove? She had read her father's letter again—two or three times. Maybe he did take his life. He refers to dying in the letter. It was all so confusing, heart wrenching. She wished she was a little girl again holding his hand, meeting Mickey Mouse.

Here it was almost midnight. Some Christmas! Not! She and Jude had joined their daughter and her husband for dinner. Lou spent almost three hours in the bathroom heaving her guts out. Jude and Thom spent the time scowling at each other until a few martinis loosened them up. And Louise had spent the time pacing. Still furious, vowing under her breath to contest the codicil, so sure that the baker had swindled her way into her father's affections.

They were leaving Dallas at ten o'clock in the morning. If all went as planned, Manny Salinas and his wife would pick them up and take them to meet the harlot at her little bakery of all places. The meeting would be brief, Louise would see to that, and then a quick trip back to the airport for a six o'clock return flight. Clifford Stanfield had pestered to go with them, and she had finally agreed thinking that he might learn something to help set aside the codicil.

Louise reached up to the top shelf in the closet for her hat—so many hats they took up the entire expanse including the space over Jude's tuxedos. The tuxedos. How handsome he was when he wore one of them. His limp gave him a certain aristocratic air, a triumph over a horrendous event … always there by his wife's side. Tugging on the brim, the hat slid off the shelf along with a cigar box which landed on her foot. Closing her eyes, she waited a moment for the pain to ease then pushed the box aside, snatching her hat from the floor.

The cigar box caught her eye. She hadn't seen it before. Picking it up, she walked to the bed, sat on the edge opening the lid of the box.

Gasping, her lungs struggling for air, chest heaving as she stared down at a wallet, her father's wallet. Her hand shaking, she picked up the wallet. Surely it wasn't what she thought it was. A postcard fell into her lap. Disney World … *wish you were with me … remember?* Another postcard, this one from Daytona Beach. The postmark was stamped the day he died. It was addressed to her but she had never seen it. Three more postcards she had never seen, never received, yet the address was correct.

Clutching the wallet to her heart, her eyes wandered to the photo on her bureau, a photo of a little girl standing next to a protective father holding the little girl's hand, both smiling at Mickey Mouse—Louise and her father visiting the mouse house. Caressing the soft leather of the wallet, she folded it back. Was she really holding his wallet? Yes—a driver's license, a health-insurance card, a picture … a miniature of the one on her bureau. A tear dropped onto the picture. She swiped away another with the back of her hand.

What did this mean? Who put the box there? Who … Jude? Why? The answer echoed in her head, her father's words—*he's marrying you for your money.* Louise fumbled for the cell phone in her pocket, took pictures of each item in the box, as well as the box. Putting the postcards, the wallet, back in the box, she returned it to the shelf, covering it with her hat as she had found it.

Her mind whirling, Louise then went about finishing her preparations for their trip in the morning. Satisfied she had everything, she went to bed, stared at the ceiling. Hearing Jude enter the bedroom she turned on her side, forcing herself into a rhythmic breathing, faking sleep.

She had to think!

Chapter 41

THE NON-STOP FLIGHT to Orlando was uneventful. Louise sat between Clifford and Jude. Both tried to engage her in conversation but she merely nodded in reply, or pretended to look at the magazine from the seat pocket in front of her. The plane landed on time and the passengers were released.

Manny and Liz pulled up to the curb responding to Louise's cell call that they were on their way to the baggage claim. They had no baggage and would be walking out the door momentarily.

Manny waved. Holding the car doors open, Louise nodded as the three slid into the backseat.

With his passengers buckled in, Manny introduced Liz to Clifford Stanfield, and headed out of the airport for the hour drive to Daytona Beach and the meeting with Star. He knew that her grandmother and Tyler would be by her side for support. Star instructed him to park at the rear of the bakery and that the backdoor would be unlocked. She asked him to push the buzzer to the left of the door and then to enter. It was Monday. The bakery was closed.

Manny and Liz kept up a lively travelogue of what they were whizzing by, as well as Florida in general. Several times they exchanged glances as the two men engaged in the conversation, but Louise, other than a nod, a quick hello to Manny, a quick handshake with Liz, had not said a word.

Parking at the back of the bakery per Star's instructions, Cliff slid out first, offered his hand to Louise, who pulled him aside. She whispered to him that she wanted to speak with Manny after the meeting and that he was to see that Jude went out ahead of them. Cliff nodded that he understood.

Manny pushed the buzzer, opened the door stepping into the bakery's kitchen with Liz. Louise, Cliff and Jude followed. Manny introduced the three in the Dallas group to the Daytona Beach three lined up on the other side of the mixing counter. Other than Manny's introduction, no one said anything, simply nodding in turn.

Star broke the ice, looking at Louise, about the age of her own mother. "Dr. Wainwright, I'm sorry for your loss. I never met and did not know your father. Your lawyer, Mr. Stanfield here, gave a letter to Manny when he traveled to your father's funeral and the next day met with you in his office. The envelope was addressed to me. I made a copy for you."

Star, trying unsuccessfully to keep her hand from shaking, picked up the letter lying face down on the baking island, handing it to Louise.

Louise took the piece of paper, her eyes piercing Star's eyes, neither woman blinking. Looking at the handwriting she knew so well, Louise read the letter. She then folded it in half, in half again, tucking the letter in her shoulder bag. Turning to Manny, she asked if she might have a word with him and his wife.

"Ah, sure. Star, okay if we go into the shop?"

"Of course."

Clifford locked eyes with Jude, saying to the group that he and Jude would wait in the car, nudging Jude out ahead of him.

Star, Gran, and Tyler were left standing without a clue as to what had happened, or what was going on with Louise and the two private investigators.

● ● ●

LOUISE WHIRLED TO Manny and Liz. She spoke in a clipped, hushed voice. "I must say this quickly. I need your professional advice. I believe I have evidence that my husband killed my father." She outlined what she had found, that she had wondered when she went to the Seattle conference that maybe Jude lied about what he did, where he went.

Manny immediately replied. "Louise, we have an eye witness that your husband was in Daytona Beach the night your father died. And, another eyewitness saw your son-in-law, also in Daytona Beach."

"Can't be. Thom?"

"I took pictures at the funeral and forwarded them to my partner here, who in turn forwarded them to Star and Benny Howard—the two eye witnesses. With what you found, there's enough evidence to have your husband arrested but could still be difficult to prove he committed murder. Evidence, as it stands now, is circumstantial against your son-in-law."

Manny paced to the front window, turned back to Louise. "My suggestion is that you say whatever you have to say to Jude on your return trip—small talk. You must realize that you are in danger, as are Star and Benny, the two eye witnesses. But the danger is following you, traveling back with you to Dallas. Please call me if Jude or Thom … or anyone close to you, becomes suspicious, threatens you.

"When you return to Dallas, not tonight because you don't want to let on about what you found, but as soon as you can get away in the morning, go to the Dallas Chief of Police. Talk to no one at the department but the chief. I know him. I'll call him tonight after I drop you off at the airport. He will be expecting you. Leave the cigar box where you found it in case Jude becomes suspicious and checks to be sure it's still there. You have the pictures of what's inside. The chief will handle the investigation. He'll have to determine if your son-in-law is involved."

Manny paced again, rubbing his moustache, retracing his steps back to Louise and Liz. "The chief will be adamant about keeping silent. Any information leaking … evidence could be destroyed. Wait, I'll call the chief now." Manny pulled his cell from his belt, flipped through the directory, tapped the entry. Turning his back on Louise, he strode to the front window, spoke softly explaining the situation. Nodding, he handed the cell to Louise. The chief wants your permission to put a tap on your phone. He also wants Jude's and Thom's cell numbers."

Louise introduced herself, answered the chief's questions, closed the cell. Sighing, she handed the phone to Manny.

"You're doing the right thing, Louise. Be careful. Stay alert. Here's the chief's direct line. Use it." Manny plucked a bakery business card from the holder by the register, wrote the chief's number giving it to Louise. "By the time you land in Dallas, surveillance will be in place."

"I understand. Thank you. I'll be in touch."

"Are you all right, Louise? Can I do—"

Louise looked at Liz. "I'll be fine. Thank you both for your help."

Manny grasped Louise's arm, locking his eyes with hers. "Not a word will be said here about our conversation. What you told us goes no further."

Louise nodded, returned to the kitchen, nodded to the three standing by the counter, her eyes once again piercing Star's, then marched out the door. Manny and Liz followed, saying they were driving Louise and her companions to the airport, wishing Tyler a good visit, and hoped to see him again before he returned to California.

Jude was waiting in the car as Louise stepped out of the bakery. Cliff, leaning against the car, opened the door for her. Louise brushed his arm, moving him back a step. "Two witnesses put Jude and Thom here. Night dad died," she whispered.

"Who?"

"Star and a Benny Howard."

Cliff nodded, holding the door wide. Louise slid in next to her husband. Cliff sat next to her pulling the car door shut.

Chapter 42

THE BACKDOOR of the bakery banged shut.

Manny and Liz barely said goodbye. All Star knew was that Manny was driving the threesome back to the airport for their six-thirty flight.

Gran smoothed the skirt on her dress. "Whew. Tyler, can you take me back to Star's apartment? I've had enough excitement. Why don't you two go have dinner somewhere? I'm sure you have plenty to talk about."

"Gran, can we bring something back for you?"

"No, I'll be fine. There's still some turkey left."

Star locked up, then Tyler drove the short distance to the apartment and parked. Flanked with Tyler on one side and Star the other, Gran stepped in the front door. Star checked the refrigerator, saw there was plenty of turkey and a small covered dish of sweet potatoes. Kissing Gran's cheek, a quick hug, she followed Tyler back out to the car.

Leaning against the car door he pulled Star into a quick hug. "Where would you like to go?"

"It's warm in the sun. How about we walk the beach ... maybe stop at a café or the Crab Shack on the pier."

Grasping her hand they strolled up the street, crossed at the intersection, then down the path to the ocean.

Neither spoke, mulling over the strange meeting with Louise.

Picking up a small seashell, Star shook her head. "What did you make of the meeting?"

"Meeting? What meeting? Other than a quick introduction, the only meeting that took place was with Manny, Liz, and Louise."

"What do you suppose Louise told them?"

"I don't know, but I'll give you my guess. I think her father was murdered. We know Benny saw Jude in Daytona Beach within minutes of when John Doe left Benny at the bakery opening. Then you identified Louise's son-in-law during the same timeframe, that day. No resolution on Mr. Wainwright leaving you so much money. No accusations we thought were going to be thrown at you by Louise. She seemed very preoccupied—"

"That's what I thought, too. Yet … did you catch her look at me?" Star said. "I don't know what she was thinking. It wasn't a mean look exactly, but something was going on behind those eyes."

"I agree. Maybe Manny or Liz will call after they drop them off at the airport." Tyler stopped, wrapped her in his arms, staring over her head at the ocean. "Star, if Roth calls offering you a job, come to LA, Burbank, Santa Monica, wherever you like, but stay in California. At least think about it. I don't want to leave here not knowing when we're going to see each other again."

Star lifted her head, her blue eyes melting into his big brown eyes, both filled with love—one for the other. What should she do? She wanted to say yes, she'd move to California. But the bakery? All the questions she and Gran had tried to answer were still out there.

"There's something else," Tyler said breaking into her thoughts, smoothing her blonde curls back under his chin. "You could be in danger. The vibes, the unsaid words as Manny and Liz scooted out the door after Louise, I don't have a good feeling. And that lawyer—sweaty palms when we shook hands."

"I felt the same. But Louise wasn't scared … or was she? She has to be a powerful woman, all that money, the charities she's involved with. I Googled her. She's a psychiatrist. Has her own practice."

Star pulled away, dug the toe of her shoe in the sand looking out at the waves rolling to shore. "Ty, when we were in Santa Monica you asked what I wanted to do next, what I dreamed of. I told you my ideas for children's interactive E-books—cooking, maybe others. Maybe you bringing them to life. With the money … if it happens, we could start a business … a business on one coast … or the other."

"Star, we aren't kids. Both of us have turned thirty. We both have started down a path we thought we wanted … there will be lots of turns in the road, I know that, but we worked hard to get where we are. Our dreams we shared under the stars in Santa Monica are coming true … almost … except that I don't want to leave you in a few days, I don't want to leave you ever."

"I don't want you to leave, but now is not the right time, is it? There are so many things we have to do first. My bakery is barely surviving, I haven't heard anything back about the screen test, and you haven't heard from the producer if he's interested in *The Little Baker Girl.*"

"I know. But all of that should become clear in January. Don't you think?"

By January? Answer the big question that wasn't asked or answered by January—would Star move to LA or would Ty move back home to Daytona Beach. How could she ask him to leave where the action is, Burbank known for film production?

Tyler turned to the ocean, fists jammed in his trouser pockets. He tamped down the anxiety of going out on his own—where? *Was it too soon to even contemplate such a thought? And the other big question—where? East coast? West coast?*

Chapter 43

Dallas, Texas

THE AROMA OF FRESH-brewed coffee roused Jude from a sound sleep, drawing him to the kitchen. Louise sat at the kitchen table sorting through some papers, tucking them in folders. She logged off her laptop, closed it, then took her empty coffee mug to the dishwasher.

"Good morning, sweetheart," Jude said, moving to kiss her cheek but hit thin air. "You're up early. I thought you might sleep in after yesterday."

"No, I have an early appointment with a patient and I'm scheduled at a fundraiser for dinner. Don't wait up for me." Picking up the folders, her laptop, and shouldering her bag, she walked out closing the door behind her.

Cursing that his leg was a beast today, Jude lit up a cigarette, poured a cup of coffee, limped to the window overlooking the city. If he angled his head just right, he could spot Louise's red Cadillac at the corner stoplight. He had timed it once—how long it took by elevator from their thirty-first floor penthouse on top of the condo tower to the garage below, out to the street, to the streetlight.

He scrubbed his wiry black scalp with his knuckles ... waiting. There she was.

Jude checked his watch. He decided to give Cliff another fifteen minutes to get squared away in his office. He dumped the remnants of the coffee in the sink, took a long draw on the cigarette then doused it under the faucet throwing the butt into the disposal. He limped to their dressing room—time to put himself together for the day. The large walk-in closet door was ajar. He knew he was getting paranoid, but he couldn't be too careful. He pushed the door wide, entered, skimmed his hand under Louise's hat checking that the box hadn't been moved. It was there, right where he put it.

Picking out a blazer, shirt, tie, trousers, he limped back to the bed slumping onto the lilac, quilted-satin bedspread. God, he was tired of waiting for the payoff. *What got into Louise yesterday? Maybe she called Cliff this morning, gave him some instructions on contesting the codicil.*

Lifting the cordless handset off the bedside table, he punched Cliff's number.

"About time you called. I didn't dare call you in case Louise was there."

"What's the matter, Cliff. You sound all breathy."

"You've been identified."

"What do you mean I've been identified?"

"A Benny Howard saw you. And Star Bloom saw Thom. That's all Louise said. You'd better get out of town, and I mean now."

"Benny Howard? Louise and I met him on our first visit to that silly bakery. He's in a wheelchair. He certainly didn't act like he knew me, or had ever seen me before."

"Jude, I don't know what Louise is going to do. She talked to those two investigators. Did Louise do anything suspicious when you got home?"

"No, just the same silent treatment. Did she call you this morning?"

"No. Nothing after she got in the car yesterday when we left the bakery, nothing at the airport, nothing during the flight. You would have heard her. You were sitting next to her for God's sake."

"Well, Cliff, I'm not running scared because two dummies think they saw something. They have no proof, but I can't take any chances. I'll take care of it, talk to Thom. We'll take a quick trip to Daytona Beach tomorrow, or the next day. We can't let those two idiots upset our plans. They have to go."

"What are you going to do?"

"What do you think we're going to do? Make it so they can't talk … ever. I was just there with Louise. They'll never suspect. It will be a total surprise. Probably arrange a little get-together with the two—the seducer and the wheelchair stoolie, meet at the bakery."

"Why would they do that?"

"Details, Clifford, details. Come to think of it, maybe you're just the man to make the call. The seducer met you, so it will be a natural conversation … about the money. But you say you want the wheelchair guy at the meeting because he was mentioned in the codicil along with Star. Yeah, that should do it. If Louise Wainwright was going to honor her father's codicil, then the pair had to comply with her request. I'll let you know when Thom and I are leaving. All you have to do is keep your cell phone charged."

"I don't like this, Jude. I didn't like it from the first—bad feeling."

"Yeah? Well, you liked the idea of managing the money for Louise, no problem there, Cliffy."

"That letter, Jude."

"What about the letter?"

"We don't know what Dale wrote, but from Louise's reaction, make that non-reaction, we can't take a chance."

"Don't you think I know that? That's why we have to move fast. You're sure you have Louise's will. She didn't pick it up … change it. It's been awhile since I checked that with you."

"Yes, I have the original. It hasn't been changed since way before Dale's death—twenty percent to Lou, thirty percent to charity, the rest to you upon her death."

Jude hung up the phone.

Snatched the receiver again, punching in Lou and Thom's number.

Thom answered the phone. "Hey, thought you might call after you landed. What happened? Did Louise read the riot act to the seducer?"

"Who's with you?"

"Just Lou."

"Good morning, Daddy," Lou said. "Quick trip, huh? I'm putting you on speaker."

"Yeah, very quick."

"Go ahead, Jude. You can talk. So what happened?" Thom asked.

"Nothing. Absolutely nothing. And, Louise hasn't said a word to me since we left home for the airport yesterday morning. Not a peep the whole trip. I just talked with Cliff. Those creep investigators must have filled her head with some cockamamie stories. Unfortunately, I think she believed them, but I can't be sure. Louise told Cliff you and I were identified, seen in Daytona Beach when Dale died. Right now I'd like to be rid of all three."

"Louise, too?"

"Daddy—"

"Just kidding, Lou. Your mother doesn't have any proof we're involved in your grandfather's death. Thom, start plans for a quick trip to Daytona Beach. The two people who identified us have to go. And, they have to go soon. Next couple of days. You and Lou start figuring out our alibi to be out of town—two days. Check flights. This time we can't drive. We have to fly. Use the new credit cards—new names, no chance of being traced."

"Yeah, okay."

● ● ●

LIGHTING UP A CIGARETTE, Jude limped to the closet, felt under his Stetson, a hat he rarely wore, but once in awhile it seemed to please his father-in-law's oil buddies. The cigar box wasn't there. Panic gripped his chest, and then he remembered the box was under one of his wife's hats, one he knew she hated. He felt the box. His heart returning to normal, he slid the box to the back of the shelf piling several old sweaters on top.

Satisfied, he limped to the kitchen, sat at the desk to make a list of what he had to take to Daytona Beach. Top of the list was his gun. He wasn't going to let anyone get in his way of inheriting the Wainwright fortune.

Chapter 44

Daytona Beach

AT 11:25 A.M. Manny's cell vibrated on the kitchen counter. He checked the display and answered.

"Salinas."

"Good morning, Mr. Salinas. I'm Detective Shepherd, Criminal Investigation Division, Dallas Police Department. The chief has been called away—"

"Hold on Detective. I'm putting you on speaker so my partner can hear you."

"Hello, Detective Shepherd. I'm Liz Stitchway."

"Good. Glad you're there Ms. Stitchway. To repeat, the chief has been called away to help with a mass arrival of illegals over the border. He assigned the Wainwright case to me. He said to tell you, quote, Detective Shepherd is a man he trusts. End quote. I'm to work on nothing else but bringing the Dale Wainwright case to a conclusion without bloodshed. The chief filled me in, brought me up to date. He said that Louise Wainwright is the only one on the inside, with the exception of two private investigators, you, Mr. Salinas, and your partner, Ms. Stitchway. You are working the case at the location where Mr. Wainwright's body was found— okay so far?"

"So far. Just to let you know, your counterpart here is Detective Fred Watson, Daytona Beach Police Department."

"I know. The chief told me about Watson and I'll call him as soon as we hang up. The chief also said that he knew the players. But he wants you to be the point man."

Detective Shepherd quickly filled the two investigators in on the very fruitful past two hours—incriminating conversations between four people—Jude Rattigan, Cliff Stanfield, and Lou and Thom Weed.

Shepherd and the two private investigators decided it would be best if they gave Jude and Thom enough rope to further incriminate themselves, make an airtight case, and now that included Clifford Stanfield. Other than the cigar box of evidence in the closet linking Jude directly to the death of his father-in-law, the remaining three were circumstantial, co-conspirators at best.

The police needed more evidence to build their case. No slipping out of the grips of the law with the plea that Dale Wainwright was dying, decided to leave this world by his own hand. If Jude and Thom carried out their plan to travel to Daytona Beach, further incriminating themselves, Detective Watson would arrest them there. The downside, if the pair made the trip, it meant the Daytona Beach witnesses were at risk.

Shepherd finished up saying, "If the pair decides against the trip, I'm ready with a warrant to search the penthouse, pick up the box of evidence. At the exact same time officers will arrest Stanfield at his office, and arrest Lou and Thom Weed at their home."

"Understood. We'll wait to hear from you." Manny shut the cover on his cell. He and Liz were to stand down until Shepherd called. Catching Jude and Thom in a compromising act in Daytona Beach would be preferable to build a case, but at a great risk to Star and Benny. In that event, a plan had to be ready, would have to be developed quickly.

A sting!

Chapter 45

MANNY DISCONNECTED THE CALL. He and Liz sat staring at each other. They didn't like what Detective Shepherd said. Didn't like one word.

"Are you thinking what I'm thinking?" Liz asked rocking Lizzie.

"Yeah. We have to meet with Star and Benny fast."

"And, Tyler. After all, he substantiated Benny's identification of John Doe, saw Doe at the bakeoff. I don't care if you ask Star not to tell him, she's going to let Tyler know something is going on. You call them while I pack up Lizzie's travel case, or better yet, ask them to meet here. More private. No chance of anyone overhearing."

As if in agreement, baby Lizzie let out a whopper of a burp, then a proud smile with a drool of milk over her tiny pink lips onto her bib.

"Wow, baby girl, that was a good one. Yes it was," Liz cooed to the startled baby, her eyes open wide. "Manny, you'd better call Fred. He has to be involved. Tyler and Star can pick up Benny. Tell them not to let on to Gran. She shouldn't be involved. Besides she isn't in danger. If Star told her anything, Gran's testimony would be hearsay."

Manny nodded in agreement, smiling as he punched in Star's number—Lizzie still kicking from the burp that shook her little body.

• • •

WITHIN AN HOUR, the participants had arrived, arrayed on the chairs and couches in the Salinas's cheerful living room. A slipcover of bright red, gold, and orange flowers protected a loveseat.

Manny, with Liz adding details, relayed to Star, Tyler, and Benny what they knew so far. Detective Watson, nodded from time to time agreeing with Manny's summation. It jived with the information Detective Shepherd had told him.

"So, you're saying that Louise found her father's wallet, put two and two together, and came up with Jude killing her father?" Star asked. Tyler sat next to her on the loveseat.

"Yes. That's why she wanted to talk to Liz and me, and why she didn't engage in a conversation when she and Jude … and Cliff, met you at the bakery … when you gave her the letter." Manny stood by the fireplace, feet spread, looking from face to face as he spoke.

Then it was Detective Watson's turn. He added the details of the wiretap, and the distinct possibility that Jude and Thom were planning to come to Daytona Beach to see to it that Star and Benny didn't get a chance to testify to the fact that they saw the two men in Daytona Beach when they were supposed to be in Dallas. Watson was careful not to use the word murder, but putting all the information together, Tyler, Star, and Benny knew the magnitude of what was being said.

Tyler rose from the loveseat, paced around the expansive living room. Another time, under different circumstances, he would have noticed, commented on the beauty of the home facing a stand of tall pines circled with lush green palmetto bushes, a narrow river beyond.

Staring out the window, he began to pepper the investigators and the detective with questions.

"Does Jude have a gun?"

Manny looked at Fred. "Detective Shepherd asked Louise that question. She said he does have a gun, as does Thom. The two go target shooting together from time to time. In answer to your next question, no, she doesn't know where he keeps it."

"I'm assuming, if they come here, you guys will get your evidence to nail down a conviction ... somehow ... preferably without anyone getting killed?" Tyler remained with his back to the group.

Liz and Manny shared a glance. Oops. The chance of a good guy being on the receiving end of a bullet was now hanging in the air.

Fred spoke up. "Yup, that's what Shepherd wants."

Tyler turned, looked Manny in the eyes. "Are these guys thugs, hired-killer type, or bumbling idiots who think they can get away with murder to get a billionaire's fortune?"

Manny didn't blink. "Thugs—maybe. Hired killers—doubtful. Idiots thinking they can get away with murder? If they were thinking rationally, then the answer to your question would be no. But money, billions, can twist a man's mind."

"I suppose this Detective Shepherd is worried about Louise Wainwright ... her safety?"

Fred rubbed the scar on his cheek. "Yes."

Tyler joined Star on the loveseat. Gripped her hand, raised her hand to his lips. "Okay, what's the plan? A way to catch the bastards off guard if they come here—"

Fred snatched his cell off his belt. "Detective Watson."

Fred listened, scanned the people in front of him. "Understood. I'll let Manny know ... and the others." Fred returned his phone to the loop on his belt. He touched the scar on his cheek. His black eyes narrowed.

"Shepherd recorded several conversations over the past thirty minutes. Star, the lawyer, Clifford Stanfield, will be calling you shortly to set up a meeting with you and Benny at the bakery. Lou, Louise's daughter, made reservations for Jude and Thom. She made the reservations under assumed names. They are planning to be in Daytona Beach New Year's Eve. Shepherd will call back with flight numbers, time of arrival as soon as he has confirmation."

Benny had been watching, taking everything in, didn't have anything to add until this moment. "Hot dog. I'm with Tyler. Let's take the bastards down."

Chapter 46

DETECTIVE WATSON AND MANNY, the point man, along with Liz began formulating a plan. Star and Benny, their eyes switching back and forth, speaker to speaker, listened. In the end, Fred Watson and his men would move in with the arrest.

Tyler paced at the back of the room, interrupting occasionally with a question. Star was a bystander in their plan, a non-participant. But, the fear that something could go wrong, the fear that Star could be hurt, or worse, never left his mind. As the plan came together, point and counterpoint, Tyler interjected his thoughts, his ideas.

Star wanted to be at the bakery because Jude and Thom thought they were meeting with her. It was possible she could help. But Tyler was adamant that she stay in the background with the officers on standby until the time they swarmed in for the arrest.

Before leaving the Salinas house, Star received the phone call that Detective Shepherd warned was coming from the lawyer. Clifford Stanfield called her cell, explained that Louise Wainwright had demanded he meet with Star and Benny Howard regarding the codicil to her late father's will. Dr. Wainwright wanted certain questions to be answered in a deposition showing that the pair had not hatched a conspiracy to gain a significant windfall from his demise. Stanfield set the meeting for 9:30 p.m. The late hour was due to the constraint of flight arrangements. Star was to inform Benny Howard. Most importantly, she and Benny were to arrive at the bakery alone.

Star made notes of Stanfield's requests to be sure nothing had changed since Shepherd's wiretap information. All was the same with a few embellishments. Of course, everyone knew that it would not be Clifford Stanfield walking in the bakery door, but Jude Rattigan and Thomas Weed.

Chapter 47

New Year's Eve

THE NIGHT WAS BLACK as thick oil deep in the earth. Heavy clouds rolled in blocking the moon. A chill filled the air. No one ventured out on the streets of Daytona Beach in the frigid blackness. No one ventured to the ocean's sandy shore.

Not yet.

A few hours remained until the hands of the clock signaled a new year, and then, warmed with alcohol coursing through their veins, they could dash out scream and yell—***Happy New Year!***

The glow of the souvenir shop windows sent eerie shadows from building to street. The windows with scantily-clad mannequins staring out with unseeing eyes, were unfazed by the frosty air.

Preparations for New Year's Eve had been made, altered with the advent of the dropping temperature. Bars were doing a brisk business, fueling the celebration. Revelers happily hunkered down where it was warm waiting for the celebration to begin.

The temperature dipped to twenty-one degrees testing the record low of nineteen for Central Florida.

Jude parked the rental car at the end of the strip mall, glanced at his cohort. "What's the matter, Thom?" he asked through tight lips.

"Do we have to get rid of them? Can't we just scare them … maybe pay them off if they keep their mouths shut. Threaten—"

"You shithead. Don't you dare get cold feet. Look. See those lights four shops up? That's the bakery. Now get out of the car and keep a grip on your gun. I'm leaving the car unlocked so we can get away without fumbling with the doors."

"Shit, it's freezing, Jude. I thought Florida was supposed to be warm."

"Shut up. We're lucky it's cold. Our overcoat pockets are deep. The stupids won't know what hit them. Now, come on. Hurry up."

The two men hunched down in their coats, collars up sheltering their necks from the frigid air as they approached the bakery. Little white lights circling the window frames blinked merrily against the cold.

"What the heck is this?" Thom muttered, peering in the corner of the window. The shop was shadowy—indirect lighting washing the back wall, the little lights at the front windows.

"I don't know. Must be decorations for New Year's Eve," Jude said irritated with Thom's constant jabbering. "You know how some cities plan a First Night party. See the Happy New Year sign—*Complimentary coffee at midnight.* See there, just decorations. Look at the dough boy. Must be nine feet tall."

"Looks like a blow-up Michelin Man to me," Thom said sliding behind Jude.

"With Star's Bakery apron around his middle?"

Thom shook his head. "Yeah? What's with the guy in the wheelchair, over in the corner? Baby New Year?"

"No, stupid. Don't you know anything?" Jude hissed. "It's that lawyer guy … the TV series. Perry Mason. It's a mannequin."

"Yeah? Sure looks real," Thom whispered leaning into Jude's back.

"That guy with Star, Benny, he's in a wheelchair," Jude said, hunching his shoulders against a blast of frosty air. "Everyone knows him. He's the cashier. Come on. Cliff told them to leave the front door open."

Jude yanked Thom in front of him, jabbed him in the back to get going.

Thom nudged the door open a crack.

"Go on, shithead. Hurry up," Jude muttered through his chattering teeth, giving Thom a push, shoving him through the doorway.

The door swung wide as the two men stumbled forward, fists drawn up in their coat sleeves for warmth.

"Miss Bloom, I'm here," Jude called out. "Clifford Stanfield."

A tall black police officer banged through the swinging door, slapping a billy club against his open hand. "Stop right there, gentlemen."

Jude took a half step to the side of Thom so he could see the officer. "I have a meeting with Star Bloom and Benny Howard. Where—"

"We've had a rash of robberies tonight. Descriptions fits you two. Mind if I frisk you?" the officer asked taking a step toward the men.

"Yeah, we mind." Jude stepped up alongside Thom.

"We're here on official business, officer," Thom stuttered.

Click. Click

Thom and Jude looked sharply to their left.

The jukebox had suddenly come to life, *Auld Lang Syne* blaring into the bakery—*old acquaintances should not be forgot*. Colored lights morphing from one color to another bounced off the floor, walls, glass cases in rhythm with the music.

"Officer, is everything okay out there?" Star called out from the kitchen.

"Not sure, Miss Bloom. These two say they have a meeting with you and a Mr. Howard."

"A meeting with me and Benny? Two men?"

Belly laughter erupted, filling the shop along with *old acquaintances*.

Thom and Jude's heads snapped right. Wide eyed they stared at the Michelin Man, his white hulking figure rocking, enormous black eyes sliding back and forth as laughter continued to belch from his body.

"I'll get the coffee, Miss Bloom," Perry Mason called out, rolling to the coffee service table beside the cash register.

Thom backed up a step, stepped on Jude's foot. The laughing Michelin Man continued rocking forward toward Thom. At the same time, the officer moved closer.

Rattled, Jude's eyes darted from the jukebox, to the white laughing hulk, to the officer closing in. "Get back. Get back, or I'll …" he shouted over the noise, the racket hitting his nerves.

"Or you'll do what?" the officer said taking another step.

Jude, bug eyed, stammered, "Back off … or I'll shoot." The strangled words caught in his throat as he pulled his hand from his coat pocket waving his gun.

Jude and Thom's faces drained of color as Perry Mason stood, stood more than eight-feet tall, his masked face grinning. "GUN! GUN! "

Startled, Jude shot at Perry Mason, pumping two bullets into his chest. Perry fell back into his wheelchair, blood squirting in the air.

The hulk, his laughter even louder, bumped into Thom. Thom pulled the trigger shooting through his coat pocket at the hulk. The recoil caused him to stumble backward into Jude, who pulled the trigger as he went down hitting himself in the foot.

Perry Mason rocked back, hands falling to the side over the arms of his wheelchair, a red stain spreading on his white shirt.

The hulk, groaning, slowly slithered to the floor into a heap of heavy white plastic.

Four officers rushed in the front door, four more from the kitchen, through the swinging doors.

Thom's legs buckled when Perry Mason rose from his wheelchair. Perry was alive … but Jude shot him.

Thom crumpled to the floor in the fetal position, crying, crying, crying. "I didn't do anything. I didn't do anything. It was Jude. It was all Jude."

Struggling against the sweat pouring down his neck, Perry pulled his head off. Now a mere five-foot-seven, Benny slumped back into his wheelchair mopping up the ketchup on his shirt, the shirt that covered his bullet-proof best shielding him from the top of his head to the tip of his toe. He had practiced standing for several hours waiting to perform his part as Perry Mason, but he was feeling a little faint from the heat of Perry's large head.

Officers hauled Thom up from the floor, still crying that he did nothing. They hauled Jude to one foot the other bleeding from his gunshot. Both were cuffed. One officer hauled Thom over his shoulder, two other officers lifted Jude under his arms, his legs. Both were deposited in the caged van parked out back.

Detective Watson, hands on his hips, scowled down at the headless Perry Mason. "Benny, you promised you'd stay back. That was the deal."

"Yeah, well, I just sorta ad-libbed. It was spur-of-the-moment, my roll on. I was ready, had the ketchup rigged to spurt. You guys had me covered—bullet proof vests overlapping top to bottom." Benny sheepishly looked up at the big officer who continued scowling down while holding out his handkerchief.

A timid smile slowly turned Benny's lips up as he accepted the handkerchief, smearing the ketchup as he tried to wipe the gooey stuff off his shirt.

Star and Tyler pushed through the swinging doors, rushed to Benny's side, knelt on the floor beside his wheelchair. "Are you all right? What in the world did you think you were doing?"

"Detective Watson already scolded me."

"But, Benny, you could—" Star stopped mid-sentence, as she and Tyler chuckled. Benny was not bleeding unless ketchup counted as blood.

Tyler stood, moved a chair next to Benny for Star. Holding Benny's hand she slid up on the chair as her smile faded. "Benny, you could have been hurt. Killed." Her eyes filled with tears. "I would never have forgiven myself if anything happened to you." Blinking, trying to hold the tears back, she looked away from her dear friend. Tyler was over rolling up the remains of the Michelin man. She looked back into Benny's eyes seeking his help.

"Hey, Star. I'm fine ... really. Now don't you go crying. The good guys won ... or is something else going on here? Tell me."

Star shook her head. "Things are changing. I don't know ..."

Benny looked down. Star was clutching his hand, holding on to something she knew was real—their friendship. "Don't you worry that pretty head of yours. You'll know what to do when the time comes. Follow your heart, and everything will work out."

Biting her lip, she nodded, swiped at tear, eyes following Tyler.

"Oh, Star, you're in love. Perry Mason knows these things."

Star smiled at Benny, squeezed his hand, her eyes turning back to Tyler. He was walking to the coffee service table.

Reaching behind the coffeemaker, he switched off the cameras he'd set up, hoping to catch Jude and Thom in the act, an act to help the police nail the case. His eyes swept the shop. *What a scene. All digitized. All captured in computer files, segmented by camera angle.*

Cartoon characters danced through Tyler's head. He had the beginning of a sequel to *The Little Baker Girl*—Perry Mason and Michelin Man save the chocolate fudge cupcakes.

Chapter 48

New Year's Day

BY THE TIME everyone left the bakery, including the police, it was 2:00 a.m. when Tyler walked Star to her front door. Both exhausted, both emotionally drained. They kissed and said goodnight. Star tiptoed into her apartment and quietly prepared for bed, climbing the ladder to her bunk.

She lay staring at the ceiling. Another few hours and Ty will be leaving, returning to California. No plans on when we'll see each other next. No plans for anything. Gran will be next to leave. She's tired. She mentioned again that maybe it was time to return to Hoboken.

A tear rolled down Star's cheek onto the pillow she clutched to her chest. "I love you, Ty. What are we going to do?" she whispered, snuffling, burrowing under the covers, drying her eyes with the edge of the sheet, only to have more droplets spring up.

"Dear, are you crying?"

Star peeked out from under the covers. Gran was standing on the second rung of the ladder looking at the lump under the covers.

"I miss Ty and he hasn't even left yet."

Gran carefully climbed up the remaining rungs, crawled next to her granddaughter, cradled her in her arms.

"What am I going to do, Gran? The bakery? Ty? You should have seen him tonight, setting everything up."

"From what little you told me when you called, it must have been scary. I don't think you should have been there."

Wiping her eyes, Star smiled. "Gran, I was surrounded by police officers ready to pounce. They kept me in the back next to the cupboard with all the bread pans. Ty said he'd bring the clip to the bakery in the morning so everyone can see Benny. Ty kept calling Benny a hero."

"Well, I'm climbing back down. We only have a few hours to sleep. Little did we know when you invited everyone to the bakery for a New Year's Day brunch that it was going to be an expose. News reports kept popping up on television about all the police cars at your bakery. Of course, that got my attention. Then another breaking news report saying shots had been fired. All I knew was that you were with Tyler. I never dreamed you were at the bakery. I thought maybe a robbery. You should have told me. I was about to the call the police when you called."

Star shifted out of her grandmother's arms. "Gran, I couldn't. Detective Watson kept saying how vital it was that everything be kept quiet."

"I understand … I guess. But I can't say I liked being left in the dark." She patted Star's hand. "Are you okay?"

"Yes, I'm okay. Why don't you sleep in so—"

"What? Miss all the excitement? I'm coming with you. What time did you say brunch is?"

"Eleven. I'm going in at eight. Make sure everything is cleaned up and I'll bake some muffins, a couple of loaves of crusty olive bread so the bakery will have the welcoming scent of fresh bread."

Gran giggled. "I bet you anything they'll all be early with the nonstop television news reports, even if it is a holiday. I'm surprised the phone isn't ringing right now. Benny definitely. He'll be antsy to tell the Butterworth sisters what happened last night."

● ● ●

THE BAKERY WAS BUZZING before 10:30 as Gran predicted. Benny didn't wait to be picked up. Stocking cap and muffler bouncing in the breeze, he motored up Atlantic Avenue. He shot through the front door Star held open for him. Laughing, she told him the Butterworth sisters were just coming in the back door. Grinning, he startled the sisters by rolling into the kitchen immediately relating in great detail the events with two men … carrying guns! Of course, he repeated the story when Wanda arrived.

Star silently went about setting up the brunch buffet on the kitchen island—muffins, bread sliced in a basket, deli-meat plate, and a pineapple upside-down cake. She was aware of the chatter around her, but paid them no mind. Her thoughts were of Tyler, hoping he would arrive soon. She was aware the little clusters of two or three, one or two, kept changing—sometimes laughing, sometimes whispering, sometimes a furtive glance toward Star, then heads bent together again. But Benny was the center of attention—the main attraction.

Tyler bustled in the backdoor, gave Star a peck on the lips, a hug with another kiss on her forehead before releasing her. Spreading a dishtowel at the end of the baking table, he set up his laptop, clicked the play button.

You could have heard a cat tiptoeing across the floor in the quiet that enveloped the kitchen. Quiet except when Perry Mason stood, yelled, and shots rang out. Hattie and Mattie screamed. Benny smiled knowing the kicker was coming—flicking the ketchup off his shirt.

Tyler hit pause, retrieved his phone from his pants pocket. Seeing the caller ID, he hit the resume button on the laptop, turned his back on everyone and walked out the backdoor to talk. Returning in a few minutes, he glanced Star's way, then stood back leaning against the wall for the last of the video.

Star watched him out of the corner of her eyes, then looked back at the laptop for the last few seconds of the take down.

The sisters and Wanda clapped so hard their palms turned red, as did Benny's face as each hugged him, kissed his cheeks, danced around his chair. Then Hattie pushed the chair to the front of the shop singing *For He's a Jolly Good Fellow*. Mattie followed dancing around the display cases, whisking a cloth over the glass. Wanda and Gran followed bringing the pineapple upside-down cake and sugar cookies with sprinkles to set by the coffee service. All joined Hattie in song.

In the back, Star stepped into Tyler's embrace. Leaning back, she asked him who called. The look on his face spelled bad news.

"No, no. Not bad," he replied, his fingers running down her arms, grasping her hands.

"For *not bad*, you look worried. What's wrong?"

"It was the producer. It's a go for *The Little Baker Girl*. He wants to handle it. Be my agent. There's a slot he's already scheduled around Valentine's Day."

"Ty, that's wonderful." Star managed to get the words out even though they strangled in her throat. His life was moving forward without her, moving far away.

"Hey, where is everybody?" Manny asked, Liz bumping through the backdoor with Lizzie in her carrier.

The singing dancers swung back to the kitchen from the front of the shop pushing Benny in the lead. "Manny, Liz, just in time to celebrate. Have you seen the video?" Anne called out.

"Yes, Ty sent us a copy. I previewed the action just before we left the house," Liz said grinning, giving Ty a congratulatory hug. Her brows furrowed. Something was wrong—he and Star didn't look happy.

Star turned away from Tyler. She couldn't bear to see the confusion in his eyes. "Manny, any news? What's happening in Dallas? Is Louise okay?" she asked.

"Yes, can we get a couple more stools? Might as well stay in the kitchen. Detective Shepherd called me several times during the night. Seems after Detective Watson's men hauled Jude and Thom out, as you saw in the video, things became very active in Dallas. Detective Watson had the signed document ready to remand Jude and Thom over to Detective Shepherd's custody in Dallas. So, while Detective Watson escorted the pair on the flight from Florida, Shepherd served the search warrant and took possession of the cigar box Louise Wainwright found in the closet, even though Jude had rearranged the shelf."

"What was in the cigar box, Manny," Hattie asked.

"I didn't know about any cigar box." Mattie added.

"The box had incriminating evidence—John Doe's wallet and some postcards he had sent to his daughter that Jude had intercepted. The postcards told Louise where he was and where he was staying."

"Oh, my. I would say that put the nail in Jude's coffin," Wanda said.

"You can say that again, Wanda," Liz chirped, her hand gently rocking Lizzie's carrier.

"Yup," Manny said topping off his coffee. "And, Detective Shepherd then arrested Dale Wainwright's lawyer, and arrested Lou Weed, Louise's daughter, on conspiracy to commit murder. Shepherd thinks Lou will agree to testify against her husband, admit her part in the scheme."

Benny piped up. "But you told us that she's pregnant, surely—"

"Louise paid her bail. She's out in her mother's custody." Manny looked at his watch. "And now, I think it's about time to call Louise Wainwright. She wants to talk to you, Star. She has something to tell you," Manny said punching the number, waiting for Louise to pick up.

"Good morning, Louise. It's Manny Salinas, and I have Star Bloom for you. Hang on."

Manny handed the phone to Star. She backed away, shaking her head. Manny nodded for her to take the phone, pushing it into her hand.

"Miss Bloom, are you there?"

A whisper of air fell over Star's lips. "Yes, I'm here."

"Someday I want to tell you in person how grateful I am to you that my father found happiness at the end. That you inadvertently gave his remaining time a purpose. And … I want to apologize for not speaking with you when we met in your bakery. There was so much going on that I was afraid to speak for fear I would say something that my husband might know I was on to him. Will you forgive me?"

"Yes … of course."

"Not knowing Cliff was involved I almost ruined any hope of catching them by surprise. But I'll save the gory details until we meet."

Star listened to Louise. She paced the kitchen as the woman on the other end apologized and thanked her again. Star looked at Tyler. What was happening to them? Everything was spinning out of control. Now they had a whole new set of circumstances. Good? Bad? No … it couldn't be bad.

"Miss Bloom, are you there? I can't hear you."

"I'm sorry. Yes, I'm here."

"One more thing, Miss Bloom. Can you email me your bank account number? The money my father stipulated in his codicil should be paid to you. It will be deposited electronically tomorrow."

Chapter 49

THE COMMOTION AT THE BAKERY, hugs, kisses, whispers of what was Star going to do, came to an end. Manny and Liz took Gran to dinner, telling Star they would drive her home. Wanda and the Butterworth sisters drew straws as to which car would transport the exhausted Perry Mason home. Wanda won the draw.

The sun had set by five-thirty and the stars were popping out. The holiday was drawing to an end. The temperature stalled in the mid-twenties. A few brave souls walked along the beach, some carrying boom boxes on their shoulders, drums beating over the gentle surf. Children, oblivious to the cold, ran laughing, pushing, shoving each other like puppies.

Tyler gripped Star's hand as they shuffled over the sand. He was leaving shortly. Star was driving him to the Orlando Airport. These were their last hours together, for how long they didn't know. But, they were determined not to be sad.

The past year had been incredible. After all, we met didn't we? A chance meeting in a diner and now they were lovers. He had a wonderful, stimulating, challenging job in California. She had opened a bakery and come the second of January, when the banks opened, Star would be an heiress with twenty-five million dollars in her account.

Yes, it had been a very good year.

"So, my little baker girl, what are you going to do first with the money?"

"Invest in the bakery?" She looked up at him, her eyes searching his face, questioning, seeking answers.

"Star, you have to take care of the money. In my short few months in California, the film industry, I've seen many make a fortune one day only to lose it the next."

"Ty, I don't want to be one of those people, but how—"

"You need help. I think you told me that your dad's an accountant. You can talk to my dad ... no, family may not be a good idea. Talk to Louise Wainwright. Give to one of her charities—do something worthwhile besides being a tax deduction. Money changes things ... changes people."

"You're not saying that I've changed are you?"

"No, but you have the means to dream big. You don't want to squander it. You're smart. You've fulfilled the bakery dream. What's your next dream, next *big* dream?"

"Ty, you know I can't answer that ... not yet anyway. Roth hasn't called. If he doesn't offer me a job, then ... well ... either way ... I don't know." Tyler had her head spinning. She felt overwhelmed. Inadequate. Incapable of making such big decisions.

"Come on, Miss Bloom, what's swirling around under those blonde curls—an E-book for kids? Study nutrition to serve up the most nutritious, healthy ingredients in those E-books?"

A big bang filled the air over the water. A group of college students were huddled over a makeshift launch pad, shooting the remnants of their fireworks, extending their celebration of a new year. Bursts of color filled the sky, cascading into more bursts, more shots into the blanket of stars above. The freezing temperatures of the night before had moderated, but the air was still very cold. Star wrapped her coat tighter as Tyler pulled her down to the sand, cuddling her on his lap. Squealing in delight, she pointed at a starburst ending in streamers. It was the last.

Still holding her, kissing her silky hair, he whispered, "I love you, Star Bloom."

Snuggling deeper into his chest, "I love you, Ty, so much it hurts. Tomorrow—"

"Shh. I haven't told you my latest idea, another collaboration besides the E-books."

"What?"

"A comic strip. Not for newspapers, but a strip that appears on a home page greeting the user … a chuckle to start his or her day. I'm thinking the first might be called, *The Bakers*. Fun, filled with pratfalls of a certain baker I know," he said hugging her to him. "And, can't you just see the Butterworth sisters … and Benny. I'm thinking of a series, pitching it to Google, Yahoo, Amazon. It could also be an app for smartphones. Maybe monetize the strip by including a product, advertise a product as the sisters cook up the next laugh."

Star squirmed around onto the sand. "Ty, it could be very cute, and lots of fun. Oh, I could tell you so many funny calamities that go on every day in the bakery."

"I was sure you could give me material. Banking on it. And I was thinking of another … like the sting last night. Include Benny's trials inside the Perry Mason costume."

Tyler pulled her to her feet, held her close. It was time to leave to catch his flight.

"Of course, it would be nice if there were two people working together, a couple in love, their desks almost touching, in front of a panel of windows overlooking the ocean, and out of the corner of their eyes they could see the Hippodrome housing a very beautiful carousel, and one particular white horse, on which perched a beautiful blonde. Of course, her name would just happen to be Star."

Star looked down, dug her toe in the sand, Dale Wainwright's words swirling in her mind—Never hesitate to take a risk that in your heart you believe in, if only you had the nerve. Go for it!

Chapter 50

EVERYTHING HAD BEEN said. He held her in his arms, hugged, embraced—the last kiss goodbye.

Star watched Tyler disappear as the airport escalator crowned the top landing. She visualized him making his way to the tram that would transport him to his gate. She stood staring as the stairs continued to mount the slope, her arms wrapped around her where Ty's body had been only minutes before. His lingering kiss, embrace.

Sighing, she turned and slowly made her way to the multi-tiered parking garage.

Pulling out of the airport Star merged east onto FL 528, the road native Floridians called the B-line to the Kennedy Space Center. At the fork in the highway, she turned north on I-95. As she drove she struggled to assemble her thoughts in some kind of order, what she had to do before opening the bakery tomorrow … a day without Tyler.

Her cell signaled an incoming call. She reached across the console, fished around in her tote for the phone, checked the display. It was Vincent Roth.

"Happy New Year, Mr. Roth."

"And to you too, Star. I hope you don't mind my calling so late." Roth chuckled. "Of course it's only seven o'clock here."

"Not at all. What's up?"

"I could have waited until tomorrow, but I was anxious to tell you the good news. I just got off the phone with a cable network. The Bakeoff reality series has been scheduled the second week in February. And, I also have their go-ahead for the new show I outlined to you after your screen test. Just to let you know, your screen test caused quite a stir. I believe you are headed for stardom, Star." Roth chuckled again.

Star turned off I-95 into a rest area, parking beside a line of palm trees.

"Star, are you there?"

"Yes, I'm here, Mr. Roth. What exactly does this mean ... the new show?"

Another chuckle from Roth. "It means, my dear, that I'm offering you a job in television. A guest host to start with, giving commentary on each episode of the bakeoff, then a weekly spot with your own show which could expand to daily. An offer letter is in the mail, snail mail, so outdated but still necessary I guess ... a piece of paper to sign, original signatures on file. A bunch of rigmarole, I say. Anyway, an email will follow our conversation with a copy of the letter attached. I think you'll find your compensation generous including relocation benefits."

Relocation!

"When exactly do you want me to start ... to arrive in Los Angeles?"

"Well, yesterday, of course." Another chuckle. "As soon as possible. If you could wrap up your obligations in Daytona Beach in two, three weeks if necessary. What do you say, Star? Do I hear a big yes?"

"I'm not sure ... my obligations, as you said, are significant. But, you'll have my answer tomorrow, definitely no later than the day after."

"Oh. You don't sound very excited, I'd hoped—"

"I am excited ... but my obligations ... two days at most, Mr. Roth. You'll have my answer. And, thank you. I'm very happy you called today."

• • •

"HI, GRAN."

"Where are you, dear? Is everything all right? Did Tyler catch his flight?"

"Yes, he did. Everything is fine. I'm driving back on I-95. I just finished talking with Mr. Roth."

"*The* Mr. Roth as in waiting for his call to offer you a job? That Mr. Roth?"

"Yes, Gran. That Mr. Roth." Star laughed ending in a sigh. Every morning since Star returned from California, Gran had asked if Mr. Roth had called.

"And, dear ... what did he say? And when do you start?"

"What makes you think he offered me a job?"

"Well, big bosses don't call on a holiday with bad news. When does he want to see you?"

"Two or three weeks."

"Oh, my, that soon. What are you going to do, dear ... you know about Roth's offer?"

"I don't know. I need your help."

"You know, Star, you don't have to work ... you're an heir—"

"Stop! Gran, don't say what you were going to say. Of course I have to work. There are so many exciting things I want to do and the list grows by the minute. That money ... right now that money doesn't seem real. Besides, as Ty said, I have to take care of it. Do something important. I'm totally drained. Tomorrow will be another big day ... opening the bakery after a holiday."

"I'll fix a midnight snack—maybe a little glass of that Port Cindy gave us."

"I think I just want to hit the pillow. You go ahead. See you in an hour."

Star smiled as she tossed her phone across the console onto the top of her tote.

Chapter 51

STAR WOKE WITH A START.

Clamoring down the ladder, she saw Gran's bunk was empty. Glancing at the clock as she raced to the shower, she was late. She couldn't believe she had overslept. It was almost seven o'clock.

Gran didn't take the car. Someone had picked her up letting Star sleep.

Turning into the back of the bakery, she was surprised to see the Butterworth sisters' van parked next to Wanda's van. Her heart racing, pounding, was someone sick? Did someone fall? Or worse, did Gran suffer a stroke?

She ran into the bakery. Stopped!

The rich aroma of chocolate fudge cake circled the air along with the scent of a fresh brew of coffee. The Wurly was playing Benny's new favorite—the soundtrack from *The Sting* movie. Benny rolled through the swinging doors to the end of the baking island. The sisters sat in a line, Anne in the middle flanked by Hattie and Mattie. Gran and Wanda were on the end facing Benny at the opposite end. An unoccupied stool was positioned facing the sisters.

Star glanced from one to the other sighing in relief. No one was hurt.

"Have a seat, dear. Anne has something to say to you ... a proposal," Gran said smiling. "I'll pour your coffee."

"Yes, a proposal," Hattie said grinning.

"A proposal," Mattie finished.

Anne sat with her hands folded resting on a pad of paper. Star could see the top sheet was filled with Anne's handwriting.

Benny grinned at Star over the rim of his mug as he swallowed a large sip of coffee.

Star held her breath for what was coming? Someone was sick from one of the cream-filled pastries. She knew they shouldn't have put those pastries on sale. But, glancing again around the table, no one looked alarmed. "Okay, what's going on?"

Anne spoke up. "Well, Hattie and Mattie and I have been talking for several weeks about the bakery, actually, ever since you returned from California. You see, whether you admit it or not, we know you and Tyler are … well … you and Tyler are in love—plain as you are sitting there."

"Definitely in love with Tyler," Hattie said nodding to Anne.

"Superman," Mattie nodded in agreement with her sisters.

"Well, we got to talking, then Benny heard us and joined in, and then Wanda. Right Wanda?"

Everyone turned to Wanda. "Yes, and Charlie too. He agrees."

"Agrees to what? Come on. What are you guys cooking up?'

Ignoring Star's question, Anne continued. "And then, as you know, Star, Mary has been talking about returning to Hoboken … something we've tried hard to talk her out of. Right?" Anne looked around the table, receiving bobbing heads in agreement.

Anne put on her glasses, pulled the pad of paper closer. "We the undersigned forthwith, offer to take over the management of Star's Bakery with the agreement of one Star Bloom."

Pausing, Anne looked over her glasses at Star who was staring back at her slack jawed, brows raised, shocked.

"Further, if in the future Star Bloom decides to remain in California with Superman—"

"I love that part, don't you Mattie?"

"Oh, yes, Hattie. So romantic."

Anne cleared her throat. "Continuing … if in the future Star Bloom decides to remain in California, and if said Butterworth sisters, along with Benny Howard, and Wanda and Charlie

Armstrong agree, we will continue to manage the bakery and perhaps begin negotiations to become full partners with one Miss Star Bloom."

Chapter 52

THE FOLLOWING TWO WEEKS moved at warp speed. Star had legal documents drawn up to protect her friends, now all managers. Gran made plans to fly back to Hoboken in two months, remaining in Daytona Beach long enough to help with the transition. Actually, she wanted to be part of the action, watching everybody take on their new roles.

But most important, Gran had to go over all her recipes with the sisters, instructing them in minute detail how each ingredient was to be added, as well as deciphering her handwritten notes in the margin. Thankfully, Wanda stepped in. Gave the whole batch of recipes to Charlie to type up, print out on his computer. Wanda warned him that time was of the essence. He was not to doddle, Mary insisting she had to check his work before she left.

One manager after the other continued to try to talk Mary into staying, but she put her foot down. She didn't want to be a manager. She wanted to return to the family now that Star was leaving.

Text messages streamed back and forth between Star and Tyler.

• • •

"Ty, Are you sure we can do this? *S.*"
"Together, we can conquer the world, Miss Bloom. *T.*"

• • •

STAR SIGNED ROTH'S offer letter agreeing to the terms, but more important she accepted Tyler's offer to share an apartment. He had seen one mounted on a bluff, near the Hollywood sign, that he thought would do nicely for two professionals.

Manager Benny, otherwise known as Perry Mason, found he could stand in short spurts. He redesigned a wheelchair for the Bakery with a higher seat so he could reach the shelves in the glass display cases without dropping a cake or a plate of cookies. Adding to his manager duties, he could also help a customer if the others were in the back sifting, mixing, cracking eggs—whatever they did back there.

Manager Wanda kept the books, as well as becoming chief of frosting—cookies and cupcakes—hustling into the shop if more than one customer entered.

Manager Anne ran the bakery kitchen like a drill sergeant, albeit smiling as managers Hattie and Mattie, flour, or frosting on their noses, seemed to giggle throughout the day.

Epilogue

Valentine's Day

"STAR'S BAKERY."

"Gran, hi. It's me, Star."

Gran laughed. "You haven't been gone that long, child. Of course, I know it's you. How are you?"

"I have big big news. Put me on speaker."

Star could hear Gran asking Wanda how to activate the speaker on the wall phone.

"Here," Wanda said. "Push this button."

"Okay, Star, say something."

"Are you in the kitchen?"

"Yes."

"Are the Butterworth sisters there with you and Wanda?"

"Hattie, here," she said giggling.

"Mattie, here," she said giggling along with her sister.

"Present," Anne said.

"You heard me speaking to Mary," Wanda said. "All here. Now what … wait … Benny just bumped through the swinging door."

"Hi, Star. What's all the commotion about?"

"Hi, Benny. Everybody, Ty wants to say hello."

"Hi, everyone. Nice to hear you all." Ty handed the phone back to Star.

"Okay everyone, are you ready?"

"Yes," they rang out in unison.

"Ty proposed … asked me to marry him." Star heard buzzing on the other end, then silence.

"What did you say to Tyler, Star dear?"

"I said, yes."

Whoops, laughter, clapping broke out … then silence.

"What did he say, dear?"

"He asked … do you *promise* to marry me?"

"What did you say," again in unison, again silence, everyone holding their breath.

"Yes. I promise to marry you."

The End

REVIEW REQUEST

If you enjoyed *Promises*, please consider leaving an honest review at Amazon, even if it is only a line or two. It would mean a lot to me—what did you like best about the book, the characters?

 Go to Amazon. Log in. Search: Mary Jane Forbes /Baker Girl. Click the desired book. Click *Customer reviews* and then the *Write customer* review button.

Thank you!

ADD ME TO YOUR MAILING LIST

Please shoot me an email to be added to my mailing list for future book launches: MaryJane@MaryJaneForbes.com

Website: www.maryjaneforbes.com/

About the Author

With each novel Mary Jane Forbes embarks on a new journey, a journey with old friends, making new friends along the way. She also sets out with a goal to learn more about something currently in the news. One Summer and Promises was such a journey. After a few false starts, the three main characters emerged—it then became their journey and Mary Jane held on for the ride.

Mary Jane retired to Florida and penned her first novel, "Murder in the House of Beads," in 2006. While she has written three short stories for children, her novels fall under the genre of Cozy Romance Mysteries.

She says her writing has been, and continues to be, an incredible journey. In researching her books she's met many wonderful people who shared insights on the tools of their trade and their experiences which were intriguing, inspiring and very educational.

A case in point, she met two new friends in writing "Twister—Ten Days in August." Because of the horrible tornados that swept from the Midwest to the East Coast in 2011 and 2012, she met the manufacturer of Twister-Safe Rooms. In the same novel, a sweet story of a Korean immigrant and his son Richard were brought to life inspired by a conversation with a new friend at a dinner party.

Writing the Murder by Design series, Mary Jane took a trip down memory lane to her parent's retirement home in Hansville, a village she and her sister visited many times traveling by ferry across Puget Sound from Seattle, Washington.

Mary Jane Forbes graduated from the University of Utah and owned and operated a computer school in Newburyport, Massachusetts. She now lives near Daytona Beach, Florida—a writing paradise.

Acknowledgements

Thanks again to my reviewers. Your time, effort, suggestions are invaluable:

Peggy Keeney
Roger and Pat Grady
Molly Tredwell

Herbert's Bakery – thanks for your insight into the bakery business. Shoppers in Port Orange and surrounding towns are lucky to have your shop. Your delicious chewy breads, beautiful cakes, cookies, pies, cupcakes, as well as your European pastries, are treats to the eye and palate.

Cover design: by Angie: pro_ebookcovers

Books by Mary Jane Forbes
DroneKing Trilogy
A Toy for Christmas, A Ghostly Affair
Love is in the Air

Bradley Farm Series
Bradley Farm, Sadie, Finn
Jeli, Marshall, Georgie

The Baker Girl
One Summer
Promises

Twists of Fate Series
The Fisherman, a love story
The Witness, living a lie
Twists of Fate

Murder by Design, Series:
Murder by Design
Labeled in Seattle
Choices, And the Courage to Risk

Novels
The Mailbox
Black Magic, An Arabian Stallion
The Painter
The Baby Quilt … a mystery!
The Message…Call Me!
Twister

House of Beads Mystery Series
Murder in the House of Beads
Intercept, Checkmate
Identity Theft

Short Stories
Once Upon a Christmas Eve, a Romantic Fairy Tale
The Christmas Angel and the Magic Holiday Tree

RJ, The Little Hero
Visit: www.MaryJaneForbes.com

Promises

ISBN: 978-0692335604 (sc)
Printed in the United States of America
Todd Book Publications: 12/2014
Port Orange, Florida

Author photo: Geri Rogers

READ NEXT?
Bradley Farm, Book 1

Rebellious love. Hidden secrets. It may just take a city girl to save the family farm…

Jane dreams of marrying her high school sweetheart and raising a brood of kids on his beloved family farm. Despite her parents' disapproval and her boyfriend's draft card, she exchanges hurried vows before he ships off to Vietnam. Back on the farm, Jane must fight her own battle with a mother-in-law who frowns on her big city upbringing.

Determined to prove she's cut out for country living, the fiery redhead rolls up her sleeves to explore every inch of the family business. Beneath creaking floorboards and layers of dust, she unearths ghostly secrets… and a rising mountain of debt that threatens to tear her dreams for the future apart. To save the homestead, she schemes up a plan to bring the old farm into the modern age and out of the hands of the collectors.

Under the shadow of unsolved mysteries and the critical eye of her mother-in-law, can she hold on to a home-sweet-home worthy of her heroic husband… if he ever returns at all?

Bradley Farm is the first standalone romantic mystery in a sweeping family saga series. If you like touching tales of young love, strong-willed heroines, and rustic country backdrops, then you'll love Mary Jane Forbes' story of finding your way home.

Buy *Bradley Farm* to sow the seeds of a heartwarming family history today!